With his encyclopedic knowledge of world history of the era, Michael Dupuis takes us from the streets of London to the halls of power in Ottawa, and smack dab into the boiling cauldron that was the 1919 Winnipeg General Strike. And then he takes us into the minds of WWI's returned soldiers and the reporters who were the witnesses to history, all with a swashbuckling allure that will have you wearing out your fingers to turn the pages fast enough.

— Danny Schur
composer, producer and writer of the movie musical *Stand!*

Sometimes the facts of history are best told with a human story. With *The Reporter and the Winnipeg General Strike*, Michael Dupuis' engaging recount of one of Canada's most troubling chapters overlays fictional characters on top of the actual personalities from the Winnipeg General Strike of 1919. It's not easy to come to terms with this ugly moment in our country; however, the author has chosen to rely on the strength of letting events speak for themselves. From the brewing unrest to the confrontations of Bloody Saturday, the book is an entertaining and educational insight into the timeless quest for equality and respect by working men and women.

— Adrian Heaps
Grandson of strike leader A.A. Heaps

Michael Dupuis in his well-researched historical novel *The Reporter and the Winnipeg General Strike* puts readers into an uneasy feeling or pangs of conscience as to the conduct of the two-sided story of the Winnipeg 1919 General Strike. Dupuis' story-writing uses an outside national reporter, William Patterson, sent to Winnipeg from the *Toronto Advocate*. His job is to infiltrate and intertwine the inside issues of the strike. Truths on both sides are slowly revealed. The reader is left to decide whether true Canadian justice was served.

— Don Kane
author of *Spies, Espionage & Explosions*

Michael Dupuis brings to life the characters on opposing sides of the 1919 Winnipeg General Strike. An entertaining take on this important moment in Canadian history.

— Andy Blicq
director of the CBC documentary *Bloody Saturday*

Michael Dupuis does a great job fleshing out the people of 1919 and imagining the details of their experience and points of view. An entertaining look at the 1919 strike from an entirely new perspective. An entertaining read. I highly recommend it.

— Kevin Rebeck
President, Manitoba Federation of Labour

The Reporter and the Winnipeg General Strike is a compelling read about the struggle of the working class for justice and dignity. Each chapter urges you to read on to the next. A must read.

— Hassan Yussuff
President, Canadian Labour Congress

Finally, simple words that put the Winnipeg General Strike into perspective for the average Canadian reader cross-country.

— Peter Warren
former city editor, *Winnipeg Tribune*

Protests erupt in the streets, police unleash violence, politicians whip up hatreds — and a reporter hunts for the truth. With a story that resonates strongly today, Michael Dupuis captures one of the memorable moments in Canadian history.

— Julian Sher
author of *"Until You Are Dead":
Steven Truscott's Long Ride into History*

The Reporter and the Winnipeg General Strike

THE REPORTER
and the
WINNIPEG
GENERAL STRIKE

Michael Dupuis

ILLUSTRATED BY

Michael Kluckner

GRANVILLE ISLAND
PUBLISHING

Publisher's Cataloging-in-Publication data

Names: Dupuis, Michael, author. | Kluckner, Michael, illustrator.

Title: The reporter and the Winnipeg general strike / Michael Dupuis; illustrated by Michael Kluckner.

Description: Vancouver, BC: Granville Island Publishing, 2020.

Identifiers: ISBN: 978-1-989467-28-2

Subjects: LCSH General Strike, Winnipeg, Man., 1919—Fiction. | Citizens' Committee of One Thousand (Winnipeg, Man.) — History — Fiction. | Journalists — Fiction. | Winnipeg (Man.) — History — 20th century — Fiction. | Canada — History — 20th century — Fiction. Historical fiction. | BISAC FICTION / Historical

Classification: LCC PS3604 .U69 R47 2020 | DDC 813.6 — dc23

Cover and book illustrations: Michael Kluckner
Editor: Aislinn Moisson-Cottell
Book designer: Omar Gallegos
Proofreader: Rebecca Coates

Granville Island Publishing Ltd.
212 – 1656 Duranleau St.
Vancouver, BC, Canada V6H 3S4

604-688-0320 / 1-877-688-0320
info@granvilleislandpublishing.com
www.granvilleislandpublishing.com

Printed in Canada on recycled paper

This book is dedicated to my wife
Christine Moore and to the memory
of *Toronto Daily Star* publisher
Joseph Atkinson and *Star* reporters
William Plewman and Main Johnson

To become a newspaperman you need the hide of a dinosaur, . . . the wakefulness and persistence of a mosquito, the analytical powers of a detective and the digging capacity of a steam shovel.

— Roy Greenaway
The News Game

Winnipeg Strike Diary
May 24, 1919

Today I visited the headquarters of both sides in the strike. At the Labour Temple, I pushed my way through a dense knot of men grouped about the entrance, intent on roughly lettered bulletins. They were men who had lately doffed their overalls and put on Sunday clothes. The strike is at once a holiday and a grave time to them. They haven't much to say. The watchword, they are told, is "Say nothing, do nothing, think nothing — just wait."

As I pushed up the long steps I found myself gently oozed over to the right of a dividing rope line by a director of traffic. Suddenly the crush dropped apart and I was in a long room, flanked on one side by a cigar counter, on the other by a rank of tiny offices portioned off along the wall. Probably a hundred men were milling through the room. All were smoking. The air was thick and hot.

Many meetings were on in the various rooms, but by the time I reached the fourth floor I had reached more sacred precincts where fewer came and went and more was done. It is here that the Strike Committee is determining the policies that later will be denounced by its opponents as further attempts at Soviet rule. I walked into a large anteroom. There were a few men scattered about. Someone rushed up to the guard at the door, who was listening intently, his ear at the peep-hole. A moment later the door opened. Out rushed a delegate. He was in a hurry to get back, for much was going on inside. Through the open door I saw a mass of men and a few women. The room — a big one — was jammed. The air was blue with smoke. Some of the men were without coats.

On my way out I passed a door. It opened on an office room without a carpet. There were several desks and a telephone. A safe stood in one corner. If Brother Bricklayer Owen had let me pass, I would have found myself right in the centre of things, for it is here that the inner Strike Committee of fifteen holds its sessions. But I was not able to get by while Brother Owen's good right arm held out.

The Citizens' Committee of One Thousand headquarters in the Industrial Bureau's Board of Trade offices is hard to miss. A large sign over the building's entrance announces HEAD-QUARTERS CITIZENS' COMMITTEE OF ONE THOUSAND. Many well-dressed men on the steps sport small Union Jacks in their lapels, a symbol of those opposed to the strike. A steady stream of automobiles, jitneys, motorcycles and bicycles comes and goes, seemingly scouting up and down Main street. Several Fords, Packards and McLaughlins are turned in against the curb with noses angled to the sidewalks like ships moored to a dock.

Things are different here. The Sunday suit of the striker has given way to the tailor's best. The powerful pipe has made room for the Havana cigar. Although the crowd is smaller, there is no less activity. There is a desk where I can sign up as a volunteer fireman or a telephone operator or join the militia or whatnot. Now and then a Committee man comes out of the Board of Trade offices. He attempts to hurry by without seeing anyone. But does he? He does not. He is stopped by Ed the capitalist, or the Hon. Bill KC, or Joe the banker, who demands to know what is going on and what it is all about.

I found out the hard way that only members are allowed inside the headquarters. After two burly guards blocked my path to the Board of Trade offices, I showed them press credentials. But reporters are not welcome. When I refused to leave, they tossed me out onto the street.

— William Patterson

Chapter 1
Ypres, Belgium
April 15, 1918

Powerfully built Sergeant Pat "Bear" Flanagan of Winnipeg's 27th Battalion was in a foul mood. There was nothing enjoyable about celebrating his twenty-fifth birthday in a giant shell crater with an ashen-faced officer and eleven green privates death-gripping their rifles.

Bear's squad was huddled, bone-chilled and thirsty, in the pitch-black darkness and hard rain, waiting for the dawn artillery barrage to be completed so the attack on the German trenches could begin. Everyone was scared.

Bear had earned his three stripes showing initiative and courage under fire in dozens of bloody infantry engagements, including mustard-gas attacks by the Huns along the Belgian and French front lines. Intense and a man of few words, when he spoke the men listened.

Finishing his last Black Cat cigarette, he leaned tightly against the crater's slope. Mud was everywhere. Up his nose, in his ears and on his lips. Ignoring the discomfort, he reached down, unzipped his pants and relieved himself. *At least there are no rats here.* In the trenches and dugouts they came from every hole and corner, some so large they had to be chased with bayonets.

An appalling stench from a decomposing horse, wedged by a shell blast into the opposite side of the crater, and several bloated corpses of bullet-riddled German soldiers floating on the waterlogged bottom of the crater had made the young men in the squad sick to their stomachs. Ignoring the fetid smells and a stomach stabbed by nausea, Bear methodically unsheathed then attached the razor-sharp bayonet with a deadly *click* onto his British-made Lee-Enfield rifle. With hand signals he motioned the shivering soldiers to do the same.

The young private next to him couldn't stop shaking. "Ready," Bear announced.

The private laughed weakly. "Do I have a choice?" Both knew the only other option was a firing squad.

Star Shells soon pierced the darkness, and a series of explosions shattered the silence. The heavies — long-range Allied artillery — rained hundreds of high-explosive and shrapnel-laden shells per minute onto the German lines. One thunderous blast after another in a creeping barrage tore apart the already tortured landscape, chewing belts of barbwire and enemy cross trenches and smashing observation posts, dugouts, traps and concealed machine gun pillboxes. The barrage illuminated the pre-dawn sky and shook the sides of the water-filled crater.

As abruptly as the shelling had started, it ended.

Next the *rat-tat-tat* of the Belgian Rattlesnakes — British water-cooled Vickers machine guns — erupted, accompanied by the whistling sound of trench mortar bombs. When the machine guns and mortars ceased firing, Bear gestured to the first lieutenant, giving him the *over the top* sign, then motioned the rest of the squad, whose faces betrayed one emotion — fear.

In a low voice Bear ordered, "Get ready, lads!" But before blowing his whistle for movement, he turned to the young private. "The shelling has softened Fritz up and we have the advantage for the first fifteen minutes. Today we are going to kick the Kaiser's arse back to Berlin. Summon your courage and for Christ's sakes, remember your training. Get over the top smartly and keep moving once you're on the duckboards. Don't worry about your backs, the moppers will cover you."

After rubbing the Canadian maple leaf on his cap badge and fingering his dog tags for good luck, he silently repeated the prayer he used each time before combat, *Almighty God, please let me make it through this day.*

With his heart pounding and muscles twitching, Bear braced himself. It was now all about killing and being killed.

Edging up into the lead position, Bear was first over the crater's lip, only to awkwardly slide down the other side. Cursing, he quickly regained his footing and stepped onto the narrow boards leading to the German lines. One step off the makeshift walkway and he would fall into one of the deep water-filled holes. If this happened, with his water-hugging uniform, heavy pack and rifle, he would drown.

When the line of wooden planks ended and fire-swept No Man's Land began, Bear continued running low to the ground, manoeuvring around mangled barbwire and shattered drainage ditches. From experience he knew it was harder for the Germans to hit a moving target. Yet there was no return fire from the enemy trenches and no counterattack.

Why not? What are the Boche waiting for?

As Bear raced downhill, leading the squad across the hellish-looking landscape, rain made the ground feel like mush. Huge smoking gaps in the German defences suddenly appeared, and an eerie silence was accompanied by the acrid smell of cordite.

Still there was no enemy fire.

Scores of dead Germans lay sprawled in the mud and strewn in the rubble of smoking trenches. Fragments of body parts were scattered everywhere; one headless corpse straddled a smoking machine gun.

The shelling had been devastating. More precise than headquarters could have imagined. All around was destruction, horror and desolation.

Leapfrogging over the carnage, Bear halted at the bombed-out remains of a machine gun nest guarding a long trench. There would be no need to use his grenades.

Without warning a German officer emerged from a smoldering concrete bunker. His spiked helmet was missing, revealing several lacerations from shrapnel. Blood streaked his closely cropped blond hair and streamed down into a blackened face. He had soiled himself and stood unsteadily. Raising trembling hands over his head and fixing Bear with deep blue eyes, he moved closer, raised his arms and pleaded, "*Comrade.*"

Remembering the lieutenant's orders to take no prisoners, including the wounded, and waste no ammunition, Bear did not hesitate. He bayoneted the German through the heart.

What Bear desperately wanted now was not forgiveness but to return home.

Chapter 2
London, England
July 10, 1918

William Patterson exited Canada House and walked briskly across Trafalgar Square. His destination on the bright, pleasant morning was the Foreign and Commonwealth Office on Whitehall Road. His trim, athletic body was framed by a charcoal-grey three-piece tweed suit, his head covered by a new derby hat worn fashionably cocked at a jaunty angle. To combat the intermittent London drizzle and sudden showers, he wore a belted raincoat and carried a large black umbrella. To passersby Patterson hoped he appeared confident, successful and relaxed. A handsome and vigorous young man with the world at his feet.

Of course, they would probably wonder why he was safe and secure in London and not fighting and dying in the trenches of Belgium and France alongside thousands of other young Canadians. Patterson grimaced and tightened his grip on the umbrella.

Since the outbreak of war he had been private secretary to Newton Rowell, president of the Canadian government's wartime Privy Council. When Rowell was appointed the country's senior representative to the Commonwealth's Imperial War Cabinet in London, Patterson joined him. Stranded in England as a government functionary, he was ashamed about not being in the trenches alongside his fellow countrymen. As the war drew on, his social life had dwindled as he avoided the ever-present conversation about the conflict. It hadn't curbed his consumption of alcohol, however, as he spent more and more nights alone in low-end establishments, far away from the prying eyes of his fellow government employees.

After passing 10 Downing he reached the Canadian delegation's FCO office. Placing his fedora and umbrella on the coat stand in an outer room, he knocked on the door of Rowell's inner sanctum and greeted his boss.

Rowell offered a brief smile. "Have you been introduced to any of the attractive ladies my wife claims are talking about you? I believe you're being described as 'that charmingly refreshing young Canadian bachelor'."

"Well . . . there are one or two," Patterson lied. Better to insinuate he was popular with the ladies than to admit all of his romantic advances had so far been rebuffed.

"Good," Rowell replied, indicating details were unnecessary. "You know the old expression 'all work and no play'."

"Yes, sir."

"About today's business. What's on the agenda?"

"There's a full IWC meeting this morning, followed by a group photograph of all members. Next you are scheduled for luncheon with General Smuts and Prime Minister Botha of South Africa. Then a late-afternoon private meeting with Lloyd George at 10 Downing. Finally, an evening reception at Canada House hosted by High Commissioner Perley."

"A busy day. What are we celebrating tonight?"

"Hardly a celebration, sir. The reception is an opportunity for senior Canadian military staff to gather, and Prime Minister Borden has cabled your participation. Officially he wishes you to assess the generals' evaluation about the war's progress, troop levels, strategy, training and so on. Unofficially he wants you to determine whether their back-stabbing, bickering and finger-pointing has stopped."

"That will indeed be the day," chuckled Rowell.

As Rowell shuffled through the many documents piled on his desk, Patterson looked over his shoulder through the large floor-to-ceiling window facing Duck Island in St. James's Park. He could see dozens of geese and several white pelicans at the edge of the island.

Breaking the silence, Rowell abruptly announced, "This ghastly war is in its final stage, and when we defeat the Huns I plan to leave public life."

Patterson's eyes widened as he quickly refocused his gaze on his boss. "When that happens, sir, will you no longer require my services?"

"Yes, unfortunately that will be the case."

Patterson stood silent.

Rowell continued, "What are your plans after the war?"

"Plans?" repeated Patterson. "I'm not really sure, sir." In fact, he *had* thought about the future. He would have to return home, along with all the others who had *fought* overseas.

"Have you considered newspaper work?"

"News — like a reporter?"

"Yes."

Patterson hesitated. "No, sir."

"I think you would make an excellent one."

Rowell withdrew a letter from a private portfolio. "I've been contacted by a very good friend and one of Canada's most respected newspaper owners, *Toronto Advocate* publisher Joseph Anderson. He's asked me to recommend a capable, dynamic and well-educated young man with an inside knowledge of wartime conditions, political affairs and the Union government to join his staff as the paper's parliamentary reporter in Ottawa."

Patterson nodded but said nothing, his mind whirring.

Smiling, Rowell continued, "You've done excellent work for me here, Patterson. I would hate to leave you in the lurch after I retire. I recommended you."

Chapter 3
Winnipeg
November 23, 1918

When the train departed Toronto's Union Station for Winnipeg, the three soldiers were in perfect health and high spirits, joking and enthusiastically looking forward to reunion with family and friends.

The next day they began to sneeze and cough, followed by chills, headache and fever. When they arrived at the CPR's North End station, they were so sick local medical authorities immediately quarantined them.

By morning all three were unable to walk, experiencing acute chest pain and coughing up large quantities of pure, dark blood. Over the next few hours, their temperatures dropped rapidly and their faces and fingers developed a greyish tinge. By midnight their whole bodies had turned blue and they were completely delirious. The next day, less than forty-eight hours after reaching home soil, they were pronounced dead with acute respiratory failure.

As the city's first victims of the Spanish flu were being delivered to morticians, a demobilized Bear was home with wife Jenny and three-year-old Michael. Jenny was petite, pretty and lively, with a fair complexion, light brown hair and hazel eyes. Before the war Bear had met her at a local dance and immediately fallen in love. He respected her reserved nature and strength and felt secure and happy with her. He knew she cared deeply for him and respected his opinions. Most important, Bear knew they would have a future together.

Then the war came. Bear and Jenny had been married only four months when he signed up; Michael had been born

Soldiers suffer from Spanish flu.

while Bear was overseas. The spitting image of his father, Michael learned to walk before his first birthday, was talking a blue streak a few months later and soon developed into a precocious and bright toddler. Within days of his arrival home, Bear was completely charmed.

"I missed you so much, darling," Jenny whispered tenderly as they lay in each other's arms after eagerly making love. "I thought you would never come home."

Pressing her closer, Bear replied, "Me too. Thinking about you and Michael and getting your letters kept me going."

"Thank God you survived. So many didn't."

Intimacy with Jenny and time with Michael couldn't ease Bear's difficult adjustment to civilian life, however, nor prevent his nightmares from coming. Something had either changed him, changed in him or both. He had lived through hell and come back a different man: moody, depressed and unpredictable. When Jenny asked about his wartime experience, Bear changed the subject, and when she persisted, he flatly refused to discuss it. "You don't want to know what I've done or gone through."

To make matters worse, the city was still on rations, and Bear often went to bed hungry after giving extra portions to Jenny and Michael. He was trying to find work, but jobs were scarce in the city's plants, factories and warehouses because immigrants had replaced the men who had gone overseas. Now that the war was over, there were too many hands and not enough labour to go around.

What particularly angered Bear were the rumours that many of these same immigrants were Bolshevik sympathizers. He'd risked his life in rat-infested trenches, fighting to protect his country from one enemy, only to return home and find another — Lenin-loving reds — keeping him from work and supporting his family.

I served patriotically, goddammit it. I damn well deserve a job.

Chapter 4
Winnipeg
December 7, 1918

Two weeks after Bear's return, Jenny became sick. Refusing to eat or drink, she complained of a terrible headache, temperature and sore throat.

A sobbing Michael wanted to be with her. Bear at first resisted, but eventually gave in. Within an hour he regretted the decision, because her condition worsened. Large, menacing brown spots developed over her nose and cheekbones and a strange blueness extended from her ears to her forehead.

Panicking, he rushed Michael to the next-door neighbours and begged the couple for help. While the woman looked after Michael, her husband examined Jenny.

"It's serious. She's very, very sick. I think she has the Blue Death."

"The Blue Death?"

"The Spanish flu."

"W-what should I do?"

"She needs a doctor *right away*. Stay here. I'll get ours."

An hour later the doctor arrived . . . but it was too late. Jenny lay lifeless, cradled in Bear's arms. The bed was soaked with blood clots.

"What happened?" asked the doctor.

"The blood gushed from her nose and mouth!" Bear blurted. "She struggled to clear the froth from her airway and began to gasp. All I could do was watch her choke then suffocate to death."

Bear went silent.

"There was nothing more you could have done," consoled the doctor.

Bear stared vacantly at the floor. Eventually, he mumbled, almost inaudible, "I saw lots of men die in the war, but none like this."

Two days after Jenny's funeral, Michael began to cough, and Bear rushed him to the Children's Hospital on Aberdeen Street. As soon as they saw Michael's symptoms, the doctors and nurses donned gloves, gauze masks and gowns and whisked him away to an isolation ward. Despite their precautions, Michael's condition rapidly deteriorated. His tongue became dry and brown, face bluish and sputum bloody. As night fell he lapsed into unconsciousness.

Just before midnight the attending doctor and a nurse led Bear to a private room with a simple metal table and chair, and sat him down. They grimly announced that Michael had died. "It was the Spanish flu. There was nothing we could do. We gave him something so in the end he felt no pain."

". . . *Jesus Christ!* Why couldn't you *save* him?"

"We tried."

Bear sagged. He put both his arms on the table and laid his head across them, as tears welled in his eyes and he began to sob. His broad shoulders heaved uncontrollably. He had nothing left.

After a few minutes, the doctor said he was sorry but they had to get back to the other patients.

The nurse helped Bear to his feet. "We'll take care of the body."

Numb, Bear stumbled out of her arms to the door, but before he could open it, the nurse stepped forward, putting her hand on the knob. "I'm terribly sorry, Mr. Flanagan." She was holding a mask. "I'm afraid you can't leave right away. Put this on. You'll have to remain isolated here for your own good and the safety of others."

Bear stared at her, then his face twisted in a snarl. "Get the hell out of my way!"

Chapter 5
Toronto
December 10, 1918

The white hand of winter had firmly gripped Toronto when Patterson met Joseph Anderson for the first time. Given Rowell's recommendation and Patterson's qualifications, Anderson promptly offered him the job as the *Advocate*'s parliamentary reporter in Ottawa. With no other employment opportunities in hand and a salary of twenty-five dollars a week, the offer was too tempting to refuse.

"If he wants to keep his job, every *Advocate* reporter needs the door ajar to anticipate opportunity's knock," explained Anderson after showing Patterson to his new desk. "Why? Because a story can happen at any time. You have to be a skillful interviewer, asking the right questions, listening carefully and observing the person's demeanour. This way you trust your instincts and avoid second-guessing."

"I understand," acknowledged Patterson. *Is this lecture really necessary? I already got the job.*

Anderson adjusted his wire-rimmed glasses and resumed. "Moreover, you're expected to be tenacious and dedicated and on a story faster than other reporters; in fact you are expected to be better than two of any other paper. Finally, you must *always* keep your emotions in check."

He paused until Patterson nodded in agreement, then concluded, "Now, your first assignment. When you get back to Ottawa I want you to closely observe the Minister of Labour, Gideon Robertson. With the country's increasing worker unrest, he has become a very important member of the Union government. Unfortunately, despite his union background and links to the labour movement, he's not

Patterson meets Joseph Anderson.

considered a legitimate representative of workers by most of the country's working class."

Consulting his pocket watch, Anderson appeared to be finished. *Thank God this is over. I need a drink*, Patterson thought and stood, but Anderson motioned him to sit down. "Before you go, here are the rules for your copy."

Anderson handed Patterson a single typed sheet with bold print.

Always start with results in the lead paragraph. Put all essential facts in the lead in no more than forty-five words. Avoid your own opinions and speculation. Remember the rights of the individuals you report on and interview. After you have finished the story, read it carefully and add what you left out. Never give up your sources. Avoid libel suits.

Patterson kept his expression carefully neutral. *What have I got myself into? God help me if the paper is sued!*

"Questions, Mr. Patterson?"

"No, sir," he lied.

"Good. Parliament is now in session. I want your first dispatch within four days . . . or sooner."

Anderson stood and firmly shook Patterson's hand. "One final item. You're new here, so I must dispel a false allegation often levelled by editors and reporters from rival Toronto papers, especially the *Telegram*."

"What is that?"

"It's simply untrue we eat staff if they miss a deadline."

Patterson managed a slight grin.

After leaving the paper, his first stop was a bar, where he consumed several whiskies.

Chapter 6
Ottawa
December 14, 1918

Five days later, Patterson walked across the richly carpeted lobby of the Château Laurier hotel, towards the revolving brass-plated front door, and greeted the green-coated concierge. Stamping his feet to keep warm, the man offered a cheery greeting. "Good morning, Monsieur Patterson. It's going to be a chilly walk up to the Hill."

Stepping out into the cold, Patterson turned up his collar and pulled down his derby to protect himself from the steadily falling snow. When the flurries stopped, the wind picked up and made him shiver. By the time he reached the Centre Block, Patterson was red-cheeked and chilled to the bone.

Passing through the Peace Tower's foyer, he dashed up the stairs two at a time to his cubicle in the Press Gallery. On his desk was a fresh copy of the *Advocate*, carrying his first story. He was quite proud of it; he'd managed to sit in on several House of Commons sessions, and despite the short deadline, had taken some lengthy quotes.

He scanned the paper's front page eagerly, but his story wasn't there. Instead he found it buried on page twelve, without a byline. His name was nowhere in sight.

"What the hell!"

Then he saw the telegram which had been lying under the *Advocate* copy. Throwing the disappointing paper on his desk, he ripped open the envelope.

```
DISAPPOINTED WITH YOUR FIRST DISPATCH - STOP
INADEQUATE REPORTING - STOP YOU CAN DO MUCH
BETTER - STOP WILL PROVIDE RECOMMENDATIONS -
STOP
ANDERSON
```

The message felt like a slap in the face.

Patterson swallowed hard and slumped into his chair. After wiring an acknowledgement to Anderson, he retreated to a watering hole frequented by Press Gallery scribes.

Several whiskies later, he wandered back to his bleak boarding-house room. What had he done wrong? His work with Rowell had never been questioned, nor his persona of charm and success. Colleagues had often come to him for advice and to consult about work. Had it all been a sham? Were they just trying to make him feel better about the war?

He sagged, drunk, onto the lumpy bed.

Shame curling into his gut, he fell into an uneasy sleep.

• • •

The next day Anderson's *recommendations* arrived.

Patterson
Interview more sources, obtain more quotes from other perspectives, provide more background. Support statements with evidence, be more objective and save your own opinions. Remember, you are not the story. Find and present the truth and do not merely accept opinions as fact, even if they are those of Cabinet Ministers. Looking forward to your next work.
Anderson

Anderson wasn't giving criticism — well, not only. He was offering a challenge. Something Patterson had never faced in his old office, where the most *truth* he discovered was whether secretaries were calling in sick with a cold or a hangover. As a reporter, he wouldn't just be parroting the words of his boss to various officials. He would be investigating and getting information to the people. This was a chance to do something important, something valuable for his country — a chance to finally prove himself.

Chapter 7
Winnipeg
January 12, 1919

After three weeks alone and in a downward spiral fuelled by alcohol, cigarettes and sleeping pills, Bear braved a bitterly cold morning to go out. He went first to Tuxedo Military Hospital; a sooner visit had been prevented by depression over the loss of Jenny and Michael.

He didn't find the comfort he sought in his fellow soldiers, however. Many of the men from his battalion were blind and deaf or had metal plates in their heads. Those who had lost a leg, an arm or half a face horrified him the most. After visiting the burn ward filled with badly scarred mates, he rushed to a washroom and vomited.

The last place he looked in on was the "acute and chronic" nervous shock ward. Most of his friends in this section had a dazed look and reminded him of the shell-shocked men returned to action who had been unable to remember and understand orders, make decisions and were easily moved to tears.

Before leaving the hospital Bear confronted the head nurse. "Tell me the truth. What's going to happen to these men?"

"Some will die at Tuxedo, others will remain here indefinitely and those discharged will likely never be normal again."

Her words chilled Bear.

After the hospital visit he badly needed a drink, and went to the Great War Veterans' Association headquarters. As he neared the GWVA office, he met up with Ed Sampson, one of his battalion mates. Stout and good-humoured, Sampson had a tomcat face and unblinking eyes.

"Hello, Bear," greeted Sampson sympathetically. "Sorry to hear about Jenny and Michael."

Bear mumbled *thanks* and, avoiding eye contact, shook hands.

After a few moments of awkward silence, Sampson lowered his voice. "Can I tell you something?"

"Sure."

"I can't get the images out of my mind. The fire, the bodies, the rats. They won't let me sleep."

"Me too. What about sleeping pills?"

"I've tried. They don't work."

Silence.

Abruptly, Sampson asked, "Have you found a job?"

"Not yet. What about you?"

Shaking his head from side to side, Sampson muttered, "No."

"Why can't we find work? Places should be jumping for us veterans."

"It's the Bolshevik-loving immigrants. Stealing into the plants and factories when we went overseas — the same people spreading the Spanish flu. I promise you, if these foreigners were kicked out, guys like us who fought for their country would be working again."

When they arrived at the GWVA office, they began drinking. Halfway through the third round, another returned man tossed a newspaper on the table. "Read this, fellows. If you can stomach it."

Sampson picked up the copy of the *Western Labour News*. A minute later he exclaimed, "The fucking Bolshies are everywhere, Bear. They are as bad as the murdering Huns. Read this rag and you'll see what I mean."

Bear grabbed the paper from Sampson and read about workers supporting the *struggle of the proletariat* and opposing the government's persecution of socialists. A self-professed Bolshie supporter named Sam Blumenberg claimed there was nothing wrong with wearing red ties or waving red flags and was quoted as saying *Long live the Russian Revolution* and *Remember the capitalist war and forget about reconstruction bogies. What we want is a new system where we will have control.* Underneath the article, there was an announcement for an upcoming meeting of the Socialist Party of Canada.

Bear scrunched up the paper and hurled it into the garbage.

"Disgusting, isn't it, all this Bolshevik propaganda," exclaimed Sampson.

"Damn right!" replied Bear. "We need to do something."

"What do you have in mind?"

"Let's get some of the boys from the battalion and teach these Lenin-loving traitors a lesson they'll never forget."

"When do you want to start?"

"Soon!"

On the way home Bear's mind raced. Who the hell did these Bolshevik immigrants think they were? Where was their loyalty to the country that gave them freedom? He stumbled slightly on the uneven pavement, vision blurring. They hadn't been in the trenches, fighting and dying for their freedom. They didn't know the first thing about *struggle*. They needed to be taught a thing or two about sacrifice.

Chapter 8
Winnipeg
January 26–28, 1919

Two weeks later, Bear led several dozens of unemployed returned men to a number of immigrant businesses. On the first day they rampaged the Edelweiss Brewery and German Club, then Blumenberg's dry cleaning store, where they broke open the front door and damaged equipment they found. Blumenberg's wife was there, and Bear made sure she knew why they had come.

The next day they went to the Swift meat-packing plant. "We want you to fire all foreigners and replace them with returned men," Bear demanded.

"We're doing that as fast as we can," the manager replied. "If it was up to me, there wouldn't be a single one here and you veterans would be hired instead."

"Do you know they're spreading the Spanish flu?"

"I've heard that rumour."

"It's no rumour. It's a fact!"

On the third day Bear's target was the Socialist Party of Canada's public speaking event in Market Square, behind City Hall. The meeting's purpose was to protest the federal government's postwar social and economic policies. Despite bone-chilling and snowy weather, dozens of party members and supporters, as well as immigrant workers, in brown fur hats and padded jackets gathered in the Square.

They hadn't expected unwanted company.

Before the meeting began, Bear had assembled 100 ex-servicemen in the small park in front of City Hall and had led them up William Avenue to the Square. Seeing the head of the column emerging in front of the Leland Hotel, most of the speakers and their supporters wisely and quickly vacated the snow-covered Square and slipped into doorways or disappeared down nearby lanes, courts and alleys. Those that remained were shoved, pushed, kicked and pelted with ice until they, too, left.

After accomplishing his immediate goal in the Square, Bear regrouped the men. "All right, boys, we're going to visit the damned socialists' home nest."

But when they arrived at SPC headquarters, Bear found the door locked and no lights on in the second-floor office. "There's not a single Bolshevik, enemy alien or red-loving bastard here!" he roared.

The men turned to him for direction.

". . . Let's send them a message they won't quickly forget!"

Bear kicked down the door, and several vets rushed in and ransacked the rooms. When they found the library, he told the men to toss the books and party literature, along with a desk and a second-hand upright piano, out the window. After the piano and desk crashed down onto the snow-filled street, they were set on fire.

As flames rose up, the men cheered and warmed their hands on the inferno. "That's it, boys," urged Bear. "These reds won't be playing any more Bolshie tunes on this piano."

The men laughed loudly, and began to chant, "Bolsheviki go home! Bolsheviki go home!"

Chapter 9
Toronto
March 15, 1919

Newly determined, Patterson worked tirelessly on his assignments, ensuring every dispatch adhered to Anderson's recommendations. His only failing was the bottle. Drinking had now become a daily activity and hangovers a regular part of his mornings.

He hounded the Minster of Labour for an interview about the country's stormy state of industrial relations. After several weeks, Robertson finally agreed to go on the record.

"There's no doubt," stated Robertson, "that radical elements are infecting the country's rank-and-file workers. What these extremists are saying is bad enough, but what they're doing is worse."

"What's so alarming?" questioned Patterson.

"Strikes, especially sympathy strikes."

"Such as the one you settled in Winnipeg last summer."

"Precisely."

Despite the fact that he hadn't been given a byline after two months in Ottawa, Patterson was feeling more confident about his reporting. That didn't stop his anxiety when he was unexpectedly summoned to meet with Anderson in person for the first time since his initial assignment.

Upon his arrival at the *Advocate*, Patterson was ushered into Anderson's office. Seated behind an old-fashioned rolltop desk, Anderson greeted Patterson and motioned him to sit down. As usual Anderson was impeccably dressed, this time in a three-piece grey linen suit complemented by a white shirt with buttoned collar points and a silver tie.

Patterson nervously waited for Anderson to speak.

"Patterson. Good to see you. Your reporting in Ottawa is improving —"

Patterson exhaled audibly.

"— but I am going to give you a chance to do even better."

Patterson waited.

"I want you to become the *Advocate's* roving correspondent, covering events of national importance to our working-class readership. In fact, you are to become *the expert* on the country's ongoing labour crisis. You'll accompany the Mathers Commission in April and May as it investigates the state of industrial affairs across the country. Your dispatches will provide facts and analysis as well as interviews. Our readers need to know exactly why labour has become so militant and why the Canadian government and Minister of Labour appear less interested in addressing the concerns of hundreds of thousands of workers than eroding their civil liberties."

". . . I understand."

"Also, before you leave Ottawa, I want another interview with Robertson."

"But, Mr. Anderson, I recently completed one with him."

"Yes, I know. However, since then it has come to my attention the Borden government has secretly authorized the country's security apparatus to scrutinize and surveil hundreds of citizens, particularly socialists and union leaders. No doubt Robertson will assist in the investigation of labour leaders."

Anderson fixed Patterson with an intent stare. When he said nothing, Anderson continued. "By now you know Senator Robertson as *he* wants you to know him: smart, congenial and self-assured. Like most politicians he always keeps more up his sleeve than his arm. Also, while he may not like you, he does appreciate the usefulness of publicity."

Patterson managed a smile.

"Remember, behind the persona he has shown you is *another* Senator Robertson: shrewd, ambitious and dangerous. It is *this* Senator Roberson you need to understand."

Patterson was taken aback. He cast his thoughts back to the quotes he had from the interview, all very reassuring and confident in the government's response. Had Robertson fooled, even co-opted, him? If so, he had been naive.

As if reading his mind, Anderson asserted, "You must learn government officials, especially cabinet ministers, are skillful at manipulating the press. Yet in doing so, he has actually done you a favour."

"A favour?"

"Yes. As long as he believes he's in control, you can use this to your advantage. In fact, when the time comes, it may provide you with the goal of every journalist."

"What is that?"

"A scoop."

Struggling to absorb Anderson's insight, Patterson sat silently.

"Now, before you begin the new assignment, I want to give you some advice."

What now? thought Patterson.

"No man can beat John Barleycorn."

"John Barleycorn?"

"The bottle. Many reporters think bars are a good place to spend time and even write their copy, but too many promising journalists have become second rate because of the bottle. The reason there are old and bold reporters but very few old *and* bold reporters is usually because of too much alcohol. Remember the cardinal rules of reporting: get there, get the story, get it written and get it on the wire!"

Patterson hid his grimace with another tight smile. *How did he know?*

He rose to leave and Anderson accompanied him to the door. "One more thing. If you do a good job re-interviewing Robertson, your dispatches on the Mathers assignment will be front page news and under your signature."

Chapter 10
Winnipeg
May 13, 1919

Under deadline pressure to file a story on today's City Hall hearings of the Mathers Commission, check out of his hotel and catch the last train to Sudbury, Patterson rushed into the Great North West Telegraph office at Main Street and Portage Avenue.

After showing press credentials to the visor-capped operator, Patterson handed him two pages of typed copy. "How long before you can wire this?"

"Sorry. Can't do it now. I'm closing up. Leave it with me and I'll send it first thing tomorrow morning."

"Can't you make an exception? I've a deadline and my boss expects me to meet it or else. It's not long."

"How long?"

"About 300 words."

"All right," he agreed reluctantly and took the copy. As Patterson heard the staccato clicking of the telegraph keys confirming the dispatch was being tapped out, he thought about the day's events. The hearings at City Hall had revealed little. In fact, it was only through a chance encounter afterwards that he had learned details about the event — an impending general strike — that made up most of his dispatch.

He'd run into Reverend William Ivens, *Western Labour News* editor, and Women's Labour League activist Helen Armstrong as they descended the steps of City Hall. Recognizing them from the hearings, he asked if they'd care to speak on their thoughts about the possible strike.

"A sympathy-strike vote was recently taken by the WTLC," Ivens revealed (referring to the Winnipeg Trades and Labour Council). "I predict the results will be overwhelmingly in favour of a mass walkout in a few days. This means both sides have limited time to avert a city-wide labour disturbance involving 12,000 unionized members and thousands of non-union workers." When questioned how many strikers, Ivens estimated between 30,000 and 35,000. "With their families, Mr. Patterson, they'll represent half the city's population."

Armstrong had provided even further information. "Winnipeg's working-class wives and mothers know trouble is coming. For several days they've been cleaning out neighbourhood grocery stores and stocking up on essential food items." She also mentioned that enterprising insurance companies were selling "strike and riot protection." When asked about her role if the strike occurred, she replied, "I'll organize a food kitchen for women strikers and families."

They spoke with calm, determined conviction, and it had begun to dawn on Patterson that Winnipeg's middle-class citizens were being far too slow to react to the coming labour crisis. They would be unprepared for another general sympathetic strike — this time much bigger and more serious than last May's. This was important information, indeed.

Still, he couldn't help but wonder if cooler heads would prevail. Charles Gray was known to be a level-headed mayor; surely he would see the danger gathering and take action to avoid a crisis. He would also realize that the strikers' demands of higher wages and improved working conditions were legitimate and that the metal-trades employers' refusal to bargain collectively with workers about terms and conditions of employment was ill-judged.

The GNWT operator's voice jolted him out of his thoughts. "Your wire's been sent."

"Thanks. I really appreciate it," Patterson responded, and handed him two fifty-cent coins. "Keep the change."

The man's face brightened. "Thank you."

Just as Patterson turned to leave, two men rushed through the door. As they began arguing with the operator, Patterson caught a few words. He paused, hovering behind a side counter.

"What do you mean you're closed!" the first man said in a raised voice.

"Sorry, fellas. Come back tomorrow," replied the operator.

"Look here, we're reporters and we've got to get this strike story out," the second man started.

"Look, I said no and I mean it. Now beat it."

The two men stormed out, but not before the first spat over his shoulder. "We'll remember you!"

"And I will remember *you*," shot back the operator, "especially if the strike restricts wire service. Then I might just send you boys across the border to wire your dispatches."

The door slammed behind them, and Patterson made a quick decision. Slipping out quietly after them, he began to follow the pair at a healthy distance. They walked up Main to McDermot and then turned west. After half a block they entered the Criterion Hotel.

Despite Manitoba's prohibition on the sale of spirituous liquors, Patterson had soon learned the Criterion was a hard-liquor watering hole for many of the city's journalists. Hoping that ignoring Anderson's warning about frequenting bars wouldn't cost him a byline, Patterson followed his quarry into the hotel and sat within earshot. *If I can obtain newsworthy information, I can justify breaking the rules.*

Over the hotel's contraband booze, the journalists began to discuss the general state of affairs in the country, the looming strike at the top of the list. Patterson quickly realized they weren't both from the *Free Press*; the first man was from the *Tribune*.

"Bolshevik-sympathizing foreigners are behind this strike, and when it happens it'll be bigger than anyone has imagined," stated the *Trib*.

"I'll drink to that," the *Free Press* agreed. "What about the reds in the WTLC leadership? It's no secret they want to wrest control from the bosses. I've heard they'll use the strike to overthrow constituted authority and replace it with a Soviet-style government."

"What the hell is happening to this country?" moaned the *Trib*.

"Damned if *I* know."

Patterson felt he knew. He'd been doing his research.

Since the end of the war, business as usual had vanished. Over 65,000 men, including 3,000 Winnipeggers, had died in four years of bloody fighting on the battlefields of Europe. Thousands more were dead and dying from the Spanish flu. Extreme suspicion of socialists, radicals, agitators and anarchists, Bolsheviks and reds, was gripping the press, public and authorities. Government censorship, orders-in-council and jailing of political prisoners was ongoing. The high cost of living and rampant inflation was hurting everyone. Returned-soldier unemployment and discontent was growing, and veterans' benefits were slow in coming. Farmers' protests over falling wheat prices were being ignored, and finally, industrial disputes were erupting like stirred-up hornets' nests throughout the country.

Instinct told Patterson something *big* was about to happen.

Chapter 11
Winnipeg
The Strike — Day 1

On May 15, 1919, at exactly 7:00 a.m., dozens of Manitoba Telephone operators left Winnipeg's five phone exchanges. By the end of the day, 500 "hello girls" had abandoned their switchboards.

At 11:00 a.m. thousands of workers left factories, offices, hotels, breweries, distilleries, warehouses and print shops. Streetcar service was suspended. Bread, milk and ice deliveries came to a halt. Elevators stopped running, and the city's water pressure in buildings was reduced to only first-floor use. Post office employees went home, and restaurants, barbershops and theatres were closed. Firemen abandoned their stations, and city police threatened to walk off the job but were kept on duty at the request of the Strike Committee.

At noon, the President of the Grain Exchange stood in the operation's Commodity Room. From a dozen arched windows, sunlight streamed in and illuminated the selling and trading pits and the giant overhead blackboards. Normally the room would be a whirlwind of activity and a cacophony of noise, with traders placing bids, recorders rushing to relay information and telegraph operators frantically shouting out orders from domestic and international grain brokers. Instead, pits, counters, cubicles and raised pulpits were empty, blackboards were clean and the telegraph machines and telephones were silent. The country's million-dollar headquarters for wheat, oats, flaxseed and barley sales was closed for business.

By evening, news reports leaving Winnipeg estimated between 30,000 and 35,000 men and women were on strike.

Canada's fourth largest city was at a standstill.

Chapter 12
Winnipeg
The Strike — Day 2

While General Ketchen, commanding officer of Military District Number 10, had more than enough men and military resources to ensure law and order in Winnipeg, he lacked human intelligence about the strikers' plans. He decided to solve this problem with a two-part scheme of his own.

The first part involved calling in a favour from an officer previously under his command. During the fighting in Flanders, the young captain had led his men in a disastrous operation resulting in hundreds of casualties. Had Ketchen not intervened, the captain would certainly have been court-martialed.

The same officer was now a member of the Strike Committee, and Ketchen intended to make him an offer he couldn't refuse.

"Good afternoon."

"Good afternoon, sir," the former officer replied and saluted.

"No need for that. Would you care for a drink?"

"No, sir."

"Good, then let's get down to business. Listen to me closely. There is nothing more insidious than confident and committed men with a dangerously wrong idea."

"Sir?"

"This strike is a time bomb. I need your help to defuse it."

". . . How can I help?"

"Before you went overseas you were a union man. As such you don't need a cover story to infiltrate the Strike Committee and provide me with accurate information about its plans."

There was no response.

". . . Must I remind you about my intervention on your behalf during action in Flanders?'

"No, sir."

"I thought as much."

"It's a dangerous assignment."

"I agree, and in recognition of this you will be paid seventy-five dollars per week for the information. Of course, should you be unmasked, I won't be able to help."

"Sir, if I'm caught, they will treat like a spy."

"Indeed. Then don't get caught. Now, do you have any questions?"

"Two."

"What are they?"

"What if I can't obtain the information?"

"I don't want excuses. I want results. Next question?"

"Once I've completed this task, will I still be in your debt?"

"No. You have my word. Now if there is nothing further, you're dismissed."

Upon leaving, the former officer refused to salute.

The second part of Ketchen's scheme involved the son of a prominent Winnipeg citizen.

"My father tells me you have a job," said the young man who arrived soon after the officer had departed.

"Yes. I have a very important, dangerous and possibly distasteful job."

Watching his reaction, Ketchen continued, "I want you to make sure one of my operatives doesn't double-cross me."

"I don't quite follow you, sir."

"I have engaged a former officer to infiltrate the Strike Committee and furnish details of their plans. Your job will be to ensure that he doesn't betray me."

". . . Yes, sir, now I understand."

"Can you handle this responsibility?"

"Yes, sir."

"Good. You will be compensated fifty dollars for each week you watch him."

"Thank you, sir. I won't let you down."

Satisfied that his strategy to acquire the Strike Committee's plans would be successful, Ketchen entered his study, removed a bottle of his best brandy and poured himself three fingers.

Chapter 13
Sudbury
May 17, 1919

The telegram stamped URGENT was handed to Patterson by the hotel's front desk clerk.

"When did this arrive?"

"A few minutes ago, sir."

Patterson tore open the envelope. It was from Anderson.

```
RETURN AT ONCE TO PEG - STOP SITUATION CRITICAL
- STOP 35,000 WORKERS ON STRIKE - STOP EARLY
REPORTS OF REDS IN CONTROL OF THE CITY - STOP
GENERAL KETCHEN HAS CALLED OUT MILITIA - STOP
ALL EXPENSES AUTHORIZED - STOP YOUR BYLINE ON
ALL STORIES - STOP STRINGER BOB CRANDALL WILL
MEET YOU - STOP REMAIN IN WINNIPEG UNTIL FURTHER
ADVISED - STOP MISS NOTHING - STOP
ANDERSON
```

Taking a deep breath, Patterson pocketed the telegram and collected his thoughts. Since Anderson was assigning two men and removing the limits on expenses, he must want the story badly. *What to do next?* First, acknowledge the telegram. Then wire Crandall.

"Bad news, sir?" asked the desk clerk.

"Not bad but certainly news," quipped Patterson. "I'll be checking out at noon. Please prepare my bill."

"Certainly."

"When does the next CPR express train leave for Winnipeg?"

"At 3:00 p.m."

"Arrival?"

"The next day at noon. But I thought you were returning to Toronto tomorrow."

"So did I."

Patterson felt like he had been dealt a royal flush. The strike was shaping up into a major news event, and Anderson had handed him the opportunity to prove he could handle a big story. Covering it right, maybe even scoring a scoop, could make his career. Was it excitement he was feeling? Or nervousness? Or fear?

To take the edge off, Patterson went to the nearest bar.

Chapter 14
Toronto
May 17, 1919

After receiving Patterson's wire, Anderson summoned his news editor.

"We're going all out on this Winnipeg strike story. Inform the copy readers and sub-editors on the rim to forget about routine news. I'm sending Patterson to Winnipeg and want dispatches over his signature in columns one, two and three on the front page. As long as the story has legs, I'll provide editorial coverage."

"Yes, sir. I'll instruct telegraph and desk staff to give priority to the story."

"Fine," Anderson acknowledged, adjusting his rimless glasses. "Two more things. I want to see Patterson's dispatches fresh off the wire, and contact Bob Crandall in Winnipeg. Advise him to help Patterson."

"Yes, sir."

"Also, tell him he'll take over if Patterson can't deliver."

Chapter 15
Winnipeg
The Strike — Day 3

Florid-faced reporter Bob Crandall reached the *Manitoba Free Press* later than usual. After placing his black felt homburg on a nearby hat rack, he wiped the sweat from his forehead and leaned his 6-foot, 250-pound frame on his desk. A heavy drinker and smoker with a weak ticker, it took him several minutes to control a violent, eye-watering cough. With the streetcars not operating, he had been forced to walk from Selkirk Avenue in the North End to the paper on Carlton Street — a long and unpleasant hike for a less than robust middle-aged man who religiously avoided exercise for fear of a heart attack.

Arriving to learn the paper's Web press and stereotype operators had joined the strike, Crandall realized for the first time in its history the *Free Press* was going to miss a deadline. As the printing presses had also been silenced at the *Winnipeg Tribune* and *Telegram*, the only paper now available in Winnipeg was the strikers' *Labour News*.

Crandall's boss, John Dafoe, was steaming mad and didn't seem to care if everyone in the office knew it. With a shock of red hair flowing wildly over his forehead and a hand stabbing the air, he looked more like a sword-wielding Viking than the well-respected voice of the West's largest newspaper.

"Just who the hell do these union men think they are, closing up an entire city, bringing misery and suffering to innocent thousands, defying constituted authority and setting up a dictatorship?"

"Please calm down, sir. There's nothing we can do today," soothed Crandall. "We'll find a way to get the presses rolling again, and I know three returned men who are willing to help us rig a wireless on the roof so we can at least communicate with the outside world."

"What about the Canadian Press bureau?"

"It's closed too, because the unionized telegraphers abandoned their keys. The strikers are only allowing GNWT telegram service related to returning soldiers."

"*The strikers are only allowing . . .*" repeated Dafoe sarcastically. His face reddened again and he catapulted off his chair so flustered he was unable to complete his sentence. "What stupidity!" he finally blurted. "So who's running Winnipeg now? The elected officials at City Hall or the James Street reds in the Labour Temple?"

"Here's the situation. Mayor Gray has wired Senator Robertson asking for the government's support to end the dispute, a group of professional and business men calling themselves the Citizens' Committee of One Thousand is organizing volunteers to replace striking firemen, normalize water pressure in buildings and maintain garbage collection, and General Ketchen has notified all troops in the city they're still on duty and must not leave the armouries or barracks. Finally, the police are on the streets patrolling their beats as usual."

"Perhaps they are," Dafoe retorted, "but only by permission of men like that starry-eyed Bolshevik sympathizer Bob Russell and his unpatriotic and sanctimonious co-conspirator Ivens. In case you didn't know, Crandall, that man is responsible for closing down our paper, as well as censoring all news leaving Winnipeg. By God, Russell and Ivens are perfect proof gullibility and optimism ride side by side."

"You know cooler heads will eventually prevail. Take my advice and go home."

Thirty minutes later Dafoe left his office. "Crandall, I'm going home. Tell the rest of the staff to do the same. There's no point remaining here, because the Bolsheviks are running the city."

"Yes, sir."

Soon everyone except Crandall had vacated the building. He sat at his desk staring blankly at his typewriter.

What to do? The first thing was to start writing. Besides stringing for the *Toronto Advocate*, he had agreed to freelance for the *Vancouver Sun*, *Montreal Star* and *Halifax Morning Chronicle*. While stringing didn't pay well, with a wife and four kids to support and the *Free Press* now closed for who knew how long, Crandall had to find some way to make money.

He adjusted his Underwood. The first dispatch would go to the *Advocate* because it had guaranteed him a bylined, front-page story — something that flattered his ego — and assured him if its reporter on the way to Winnipeg couldn't do the job, he would replace him.

However, given his position at the *Free Press* and Dafoe's feelings about the strike, he would have to be careful providing information about the walkout and, if he took over the assignment, writing anything supportive about the strike and its leaders.

After finishing the dispatch, he grabbed the phone off its stand-up cradle to call his wife and explain why he wouldn't be home for supper. Rotating the crank handle and picking up the earpiece, he tapped impatiently on his desk, waiting for the *Free Press* switchboard girl to respond. When the ringer remained silent and the operator didn't answer or connect him, he realized there was no operator . . . anywhere. The hello girls had left the city's five exchanges first thing in the morning.

Given to tantrums — though usually controlled — and rages less so, Crandall squeezed the earpiece hard enough to turn his knuckles white, swivelled in his chair and angrily kicked over his wastebasket. "Christ Almighty!" he swore out loud and slammed the desk. "No phones. No newspapers. No telegrams. No streetcars. *What the hell is next?*"

The last thing he did before leaving the newsroom was to reach for the bottle of whisky in his desk and take a very long swig.

Chapter 16
Winnipeg
The Strike — Day 4

Despite a pounding hangover, Bear left the apartment to go to the CV Café for lunch. Walking through Forte Rouge to downtown, he encountered horse-drawn rigs delivering milk from Crescent Creamery, bread from Parnell's and ice from Arctic.

The drivers had special notices on the rigs indicating PERMITTED BY AUTHORITY OF STRIKE COMMITTEE. Without these, the drivers would be attacked as scabs and have their rigs damaged, but the signs also made it look like the Strike Committee was now in control of the city. *This is dead wrong,* thought Bear, *like having the enlisted men in charge of the officers.*

Approaching one of the orange Crescent Creamery wagons, Bear blocked the way and challenged the bearded driver. "Don't you know the reds are behind the strike and causing all the trouble?"

"Look, mister," said the rangy, flat-capped dairyman, "I'm only doing my job." When Bear didn't budge, the driver stood up in the rig. His large forearms were tattooed and he had blacksmith's biceps. He gave Bear a threatening stare. "If you've got a beef, take it up with my boss. Now, get the hell out of the way."

"Piss off!" yelled Bear and stormed away.

Ten minutes later he was at Portage and Main. The usually busy intersection was quiet now, the only traffic a few automobiles coming up Main from the Industrial Bureau. He walked up Main to the CV Café, but finding it closed, headed to the Venice restaurant. On his way he passed the *Tribune*. It too was closed, and the bulletin board, normally displaying front page news in the large plate-glass window, was empty.

At the Venice, Bear spotted another striker permit card in the restaurant's front window, but entered despite the sign. With worn hardwood floors and a linoleum-covered counter that had seen better days, the Venice was popular with working men. The smell of strong coffee mingled with the odour of stale cigarettes, and although it was mid-morning, a smoky haze hung from the tin ceiling, where two circular fans slowly rotated with a ticking sound. It was nearly inaudible over the sound of heated conversation — the place was packed.

The Venice was so full Bear was forced to take a back table. A surly waiter with wire-rimmed glasses approached and, wiping his hands on a soiled apron, asked, "What can I get you, mister?"

"A ham sandwich and some pie and a coffee?"

"Okay. Can I see your card?"

"Card?"

"Your union card. Can't serve you without one."

"You kidding me?" Bear said, his mood quickly darkening. "I've got to have a damn union card to get something to eat?"

"Look, I don't make the bloody rules. No card, no service. Now, I've got other customers waiting," he barked and walked away.

Bear was aware everyone was staring. He stood and stomped to the café's entrance. When he reached the front door, the veins in his neck were standing out and his face was flushed. He grabbed the Strike Committee's sign from the window and tore it into shreds. "Take your permit and shove it, you Bolshevik-loving bastards!"

Chapter 17
Winnipeg
The Strike — Day 5

The CPR express from Sudbury crossed over the Louise Bridge, slowed down through Point Douglas and entered Union Station. Patterson disembarked, made his way through the busy arrivals area and exited onto Higgins Avenue, where he walked the short distance to the Royal Alexandra Hotel.

He preferred the Alex for several reasons. It was one of the city's few luxury accommodations. Most federal officials, as well as Winnipeg's government, professional and business elite, patronized the hotel. Most importantly, it was only a few blocks from City Hall, the Labour Temple and Central Police Station — all part of his new beat.

He was in for an unexpected and unpleasant surprise, however. As he arrived at the hotel, there were no green-coated and smartly capped doormen at the front entrance to greet him. Inside, no sign of bellboys, barbers or shoeshine boys. Moreover, he soon learned there was also no hot water, newspapers, elevator or room service, and when he enquired about meals, he was told the Selkirk Room was without waiters. Regrettably, Winnipeg's finest dining room had been reduced to a cafeteria where guests were served sandwiches and provided with cutlery wrapped up in paper napkins.

There was more bad news. The hotel was almost full, and without a reservation Patterson had to settle for a closet-like room on the hotel's top floor. With barely enough space for the bed, a two-drawer chest and a night table, the room's only redeeming feature was a small but intricate wrought-iron balcony providing relief from the hot and humid weather.

Patterson sighed and mentally steeled himself for an uncomfortable stay. He unpacked the meagre collection of clothes he'd brought with him into the room's chest, placing his diary and a bottle of whisky at the back of the bottom drawer.

• • •

Bob Crandall was waiting for Patterson in one of the lobby's comfortable leather club chairs. Glancing around nervously, he offered Patterson a quick handshake and in a lowered voice said, "Let's go somewhere else."

Soon they were in the Criterion, where Crandall signalled the bartender for two whiskies. Patterson thought about Anderson's advice, *don't mix drinking and reporting*, but didn't refuse the gesture.

"How long have you been with the *Advocate*?" Crandall asked.

"Six months."

"How long reporting?"

"Six months."

"Well, you sure have landed a big story for a greenhorn, haven't you?"

Eager to get to the point, Patterson replied, "You bet. Speaking of the strike, what's happening here?"

"Too bad I can't give you a straight answer." Crandall paused and Patterson got the feeling he was choosing his words carefully. "I've lived here damn near my whole life and never seen a tie-up like this before, including the one last May with the city workers. We've had plenty of strikes before, and

I've covered them all — in 1901 by CPR trackmen, the 1902 CNR strike, in 1906 the Winnipeg Railway fight and the 1911 Great West Saddlery Company dispute. Most ended up a turkey shoot for the employer."

"How come?"

"After several days of picketing and no pay, the workers usually caved or got their heads bashed in by out-of-town strikebreakers, detective agents or the police. If strong-arm tactics didn't work, the employers resorted to worker dismissals, lockouts, civil damage lawsuits or other legal means to stop picketing and break the strike. To top it off, the courts always sided with the companies, leaving the strikers empty-handed and bitter."

Crandall downed his glass and called for another. "So far there are two unique things about this strike. First, there's been virtually no picketing. Second, the number of workers involved. The *Labour News* claims between 30,000 and 35,000. Given there are only 12,000 total card-carrying union members in the city, this means thousands of non-unionized men and women have joined in sympathy."

"Didn't that happen last May in the civic workers' strike?"

"Nope. Last summer's tie-up involved only unionized workers. The WTLC gradually called out member unions in 'sympathy' with municipal employees. It's very different this time."

"Why?"

"Thousands of non-union workers have joined the strike to support the demands of the striking metal and construction tradespeople for better working conditions, improved wages and collective bargaining."

"I've heard the owners of the big three ironworks companies don't want to bargain collectively."

"That's right."

"Seems backward, as collective bargaining is an accepted practice in the country."

"Winnipeg's ironmasters prefer to operate by divide and conquer. Collective bargaining with metal workers through their new Metal Trades Council would lessen their power and control."

"Is there solidarity among the metal-trades workers?"

"Maybe, but solidarity is not the Promised Land."

"What do you mean?"

"C'mon, Patterson. Things won't seem so rosy when folks start missing paydays."

"What about strike pay?"

"Not much, and only for WTLC members. Five bucks a week, starting when the strike is two weeks old."

"All right."

"What else do you want to know?"

"Who are the key people behind the strike?"

"Bob Russell and Bill Ivens."

"I've met Ivens. What's Russell like?"

"Well, nobody's ever called him sweet. If you want the truth, I think he's overconfident and frequently sandpapers people who don't agree with him. I once heard one of the members in his own local say, 'Too often Bob goes to bed with more enemies than he started with in the morning'."

"Who else is important?"

"Senator Robertson, General Ketchen and Donald Mac-Pherson."

"Isn't Robertson in Ottawa?"

"Not any more. He's on his way to Winnipeg."

"That's interesting. He settled the strike last year. Can he do it again?"

"I doubt it."

"Why not?"

"Times have changed. Last year's strike occurred in pretty unusual circumstances."

"How so?"

"With the war in Europe still on, strikers had the advantage, especially when thousands of railway workers threatened to walk off in support. The sympathetic-strike tactic was effective then, but not now."

"Why not?"

"The war's over and the government knows the WTLC's position is weaker. Fear of Bolshevism is also a factor. It's scaring the hell out of employers, the government and the public. In fact, many believe reds now control the WTLC leadership and are recruiting immigrants to their cause."

"All right, what about Ketchen?"

"He's in charge of the local military district and has mobilized hundreds of militia to preserve 'law and order'."

"What do the returned men think of him?"

"I've heard he commands the respect of the officers, but many enlisted men would gladly strangle him twice a day."

"Why is MacPherson important?"

"He's the city's Chief Constable. The police shouldn't be unionized, but against the wishes of the Police Commission they are associated with the WTLC. Officers voted overwhelmingly to join this strike and would've walked off in sympathy when it began, but the Strike Committee 'requested' them to remain on duty. MacPherson claims his men are prepared to enforce law and order and protect property. The Strike Committee can call them out at any time."

"Where's their loyalty?"

"Good question. More importantly, if they join the strike, how would you like to face off against 200 armed cops?"

• • •

Draining his second whisky, Crandall figured he had given Patterson enough. *As long as he's on the story*, thought Crandall, *there will be less work for me. Best to not share any more information and certainly not tip him off about Alfred Andrews.* "Anything else you need?"

"No, Bob. I get the picture. Thanks for the rundown."

"Happy to help a fellow journalist."

Chapter 18
Winnipeg
The Strike — Day 5

Patterson needed to reconnoiter his beat. He walked south on Main to Rupert Avenue, turned east and soon was in front of the iron-gated and fortress-like Central Police Station. The grey building was three storeys, but large basement windows gave the appearance of another floor; the cells and drunk tank occupied the entire top floor. Over the front entrance and carved into the limestone lintel was the city's motto, COMMERCE PRUDENCE INDUSTRY.

Patterson wondered if the strikers agreed with the epithet.

Hoping that Donald MacPherson would be available for an interview, Patterson crossed the street and entered the station.

"I'm William Patterson with the *Toronto Advocate*," he announced to the desk sergeant and handed over his press card. "Is it possible to speak to the Chief Constable?"

"Wait here," came the reply.

In less than two minutes Patterson was face to face with the rugged-looking MacPherson.

"I'm a very busy man, Mr. Patterson."

"I understand."

"One question is all you get."

Thinking quickly, Patterson said, "There's a rumour there are foreigners on the Strike Committee. Is this true?"

"No. Without exception all are Canadians or English."

"No reds or Bolsheviks?"

"None!"

"Will the police force —"

"That's all I have to say, Mr. Patterson."

"All right. Thank you."

The next location was the Labour Temple on James Avenue. Arriving at the four-storey yellow-brick structure, Patterson thought he had stumbled upon a full-fledged bicycle meet. Hundreds of bikes were leaning on the building and nearby trees or being held up by workers. Walking by small groups of men and a few women gathered on the sidewalk and the front steps, Patterson heard most speaking English, though he also detected a few European languages. While most of the strikers wore the trademark worker's flat cap or Lenin-like train conductor's hat, the odd bowler or Panama hat was also visible.

Patterson pushed up the long front steps and, along with several men in work clothes, was oozed over to the right of a dividing rope by a traffic director. The crush of people suddenly dropped off, and he found himself in a well-lit, long room, flanked on one side by a cigar counter, on the other by a rank of small offices partitioned off along the wall. Close to 100 men were milling through the room. All were smoking and the air was thick and hot.

Patterson turned to a man holding a clipboard. "Where can I find Reverend William Ivens?"

"He's working on the newspaper."

"Where?"

"Go along the hallway, past the auditorium, and take the stairs to the basement."

"Thanks." As he passed the auditorium Patterson could hear singers accompanied by an accordion and piano. A choir was nearing the end of a well-known labour song.

*When the union's inspiration through the workers'
blood shall run,
There can be no power greater anywhere beneath the sun,
Yet what force on earth is weaker than the feeble
strength of one?
But the union makes us strong.
Solidarity forever, for the union makes us strong.*

Patterson shook his head. *Was this staged for me?*

He found Ivens seated at a beat-up table, busily writing on several sheets of paper. The *Labour News* editor was fair-haired, clean-shaven and had wide blue eyes and black, bushy eyebrows. He was in shirtsleeves and despite the heat was still wearing his minister's collar.

Ivens looked up. "Mr. Patterson, we meet again. Please sit down."

"Thank you," replied Patterson and took out his notepad.

"I'll be glad to have a little talk with you, but it'll have to be brief because I'm preparing tomorrow's paper, and there's a lot to write about. I've some linotype machines running as we speak. We're fortunate to have volunteer union stereotypers and Web pressmen helping us compose the strike bulletin over at the Winnipeg Printing Company. So much is happening now."

Patterson nodded in agreement. "Can I have a few comments for *Advocate* readers?"

"All right," relented Ivens, but before Patterson could ask his first question, Ivens said, "Of course you know all three dailies have stopped."

"I do. What about public scrutiny and freedom of the press?"

"As a journalist I do appreciate your concern about these issues, but realistically, they'll be down for only a short time. In comparison, for years they've been shouting their heads off to suppress other papers telling the truth, and workers have been the victims of constant mistruths, fabrications and omissions. I think it's only fair for a few days that the real enemies of freedom and truth are muzzled and Winnipeggers are given some honest press about our side."

"Are you telling me the *Free Press*, *Tribune* and *Telegram* have been lying about the workers and their unions?"

"Well, Mr. Patterson, one of the men put it to me this way: 'Reverend, it isn't what we don't know, it's what we know that ain't so that gives us so much trouble now'."

"May I quote you on this?"

"Certainly."

"Have you anything you would like to say to the people in the East?"

"How could you get it out of here if I did give it to you?"

Taken aback, Patterson replied, "I don't understand."

"No newspaper matter can leave Winnipeg unless it has my approval as head of the press committee. None has gone out yet. In fact, I haven't written any myself for the outside but will whenever I get time."

Patterson put down his notepad.

"Perhaps there is a way I can manage to get your copy out. Under certain conditions."

"What conditions?"

"I can arrange for you to wire 600 words daily to your paper, under your signature, but with my OK and provided the copy is read and passed by the Strike Committee. Also, you must wire it to the *New York Call*, a labour paper in Butte, Montana, and probably a labour paper in Toronto, too. That's the best I can do. Certainly, though, you're free to take your copy and leave the city with it. Perhaps you can wire it from Brandon or go south across the border to the States and telegraph it from there."

Thinking quickly, Patterson replied, "I'll consider your offer. You know what they say — 'never miss a deadline'."

Ivens sensed Patterson's hesitation. "I realize your indecision over these conditions, but your paper and its readers should know the only reason the Strike Committee appointed a censorship board was to respond to repeated complaints from members of the Great War Veterans' Association about Winnipeg's daily newspapers and American wire services not telling the truth in certain articles. As you know, in the newspaper business the correction of false information rarely catches up with the earlier erroneous front page story, but at least the reader knows a mistake has been made. However, when the press and wire services didn't retract rumours, unproven allegations and outright lies about the strike, we had no choice but to screen their publications."

"I'll see what I can do," Patterson offered and pocketed his notepad.

As they stood and shook hands, Ivens inquired, "Are you a religious man?"

"Well, I don't go to church every Sunday or get down on my knees to pray every night, but I do believe in God."

"That's not always good enough, Mr. Patterson," insisted Ivens, his eyes burning with extraordinary determination. "While we all benefit from believing in Him, at times we're given a moral responsibility to do more with our faith. We must act."

"You believe this strike is such a time?"

"Indeed it is. Everyone cares about injustice."

As he walked back to the Alex, Patterson knew Anderson would never accept a censored dispatch, and neither Winnipeg nor Brandon telegraph service was available to the press. But if he didn't find a way to get the interview to the paper, Anderson would likely give the assignment to Crandall. Forgoing the temptation to decide over a drink, Patterson went straight to Union Station and purchased a ticket on the Soo Line Express.

Chapter 19
Thief River Falls, Minnesota
May 18, 1919

"Ticket, sir," announced the conductor soon after the train left Winnipeg.

Handing it over, Patterson said, "Do you know where the telegraph office is across the border in Noyes?"

"Not far from the train station, but it's closed now."

"Closed?"

"You'll have to go down to Thief River Falls, to the Western Union Telegraph office."

"How far is it?"

"Another two hours."

"Two hours!" complained Patterson.

"Yes, sir."

"Not your fault. Will you let me know when we get there?"

"Certainly."

Patterson flipped open his notepad, made a few changes and read over his dispatch.

```
Special to The Advocate by Staff Correspondent
   Copyright 1919, by The Toronto Advocate
     Thief River Falls, Minnesota, May 18

I don't exactly know where Thief River
Falls is, except that it is somewhere
down in Minnesota. I came into it late
```

tonight. There was one alternative to
coming down here. This alternative was
proposed earlier today in Winnipeg by
Rev. William Ivens, editor of the Western Labour News, published as a daily
during the strike. Mr. Ivens is also head
of the press committee of strikers and
indicated your correspondent could write
a by-lined report subject to censorship
before being wired to the Advocate.

I found Ivens in an inside room in
the Labour Temple surrounded by many
comrades talking and working. I had seen
him earlier in the week, when he was giving evidence before the Mathers Commission
on Industrial Relations. I had also had a
chat with him then. Neither his evidence
nor his talk was more ultra-radical than
much of what I heard in other Western
cities.

Here are remarks given by Ivens to your
correspondent.

Ivens — I do not want to win the strike unless our cause is just. The world is hearing
of bloodshed and rioting in Winnipeg that
never had occurred. There have been no cases
in the Police Courts of striker disorder
and there has been less crime in the last
six days than at any time during the last
six months.

Have you any fear that if the strike is
prolonged or other incitements as you see
them are offered, that the extreme or

rowdy element will sweep away the present
leadership?

Ivens — No, the men are keeping cool and
taking our advice to win by simply doing
nothing. We are telling them to just eat,
sleep, play, love, laugh and look at the
sun. This is the greatest strike ever put
on in Winnipeg and it can be made the
greatest victory if every striker does
absolutely nothing. Our advice for the
present is in a lawful, orderly and perfectly constitutional way — do nothing.

How about the unionizing of the firemen,
police and waterworks employees? Do you
think that's justifiable and in the public
interest?

Ivens — Certainly. It is the fundamental
right of all workmen to organize and gain
their ends by constitutional means.

Is it legal for postal employees to strike?

Ivens — Quite legitimate.

And what is the great ultimate?

Ivens — The substitution of the industrial
system for use.

Can you gain this by constitutional means?

Ivens — I think so. I am against violent
means. If the strikers go wrong, if they

```
insist on anything more than their rights,
I am prepared to fight them.
```

The *Advocate*'s news editor rushed Patterson's wire to Anderson. "Patterson's dispatch just came in."

"From Winnipeg?"

"No. From Thief River Falls."

"Where's that?"

"In Minnesota, about 130 miles south of Winnipeg."

"That's odd. Let me see it."

Anderson read the dispatch. "It's a good piece. Run it on tomorrow's front page."

"Under his byline?"

"Not yet."

Chapter 20
Winnipeg
The Strike — Day 6

"How was your cross-border trip to Minnesota on the Soo Line express?" Crandall asked jokingly.

Running a hand across his beard stubble, a ragged-looking Patterson grumbled, "A pain in the ass!" As Crandall ordered drinks from the Criterion's bartender, Patterson rubbed his eyes, wondering where to start.

"C'mon, tell me what happened."

Quickly downing his whisky, Patterson replied, "Before the train reached Pembina, the conductor warned me the telegraph office in Noyes would be closed, so I had to stay on board for another two hours down to Thief River Falls to file my story. Then I was forced to stay overnight in a fleabag hotel run by a man as crazy as a bag full of hammers. To top things off, I had to get up in the middle of the night to make the 3:00 a.m. through train from Minneapolis to Winnipeg."

Patterson came up for air. "Maybe I shouldn't complain, though."

"Why not?"

"I could see the bumpy roads and wheel tracks and can't imagine what it would've been like to jolt down that far and back in a Ford."

"At least you didn't miss a deadline."

"Right. So — any developments here?"

"Some."

"Go ahead. I'm listening."

"A Citizens' Committee of One Thousand has been formed to provide volunteers to operate public utilities and essential services. However, its real purpose is to break the strike."

"Who's in it?"

"Mostly members of the local Board of Trade; Winnipeg Bar; Manitoba Grocers, Manufacturers and Retail Merchants' Associations; Grain Exchange and so on, but . . ."

"But what?"

"There's no membership list."

"What? Why not?"

"The names are being kept secret."

"So they want to be bold but not accountable. Is that it?"

"I guess so."

"Have you tried to get names?"

"Absolutely. I went to the Citizens' headquarters. They're using Board of Trade offices in the Industrial Bureau, but they wouldn't let me in, so I waited until a few fellows I recognized were leaving. I spotted a lawyer I knew and asked him about membership."

"What did he say?"

"Nothing. He stonewalled me."

"What about the other fellows?"

"Well-heeled white-collar guys — you know, office managers, insurance and real estate agents, bankers and lawyers. Model law-abiding citizens. What the strikers call *capitalists*."

"Anything else about the organization?"

"I did hear this morning from a *Telegram* reporter there's a thirty-man executive committee. But he couldn't, or wouldn't, provide names. He did mention that one of the city's top lawyers with connections to Ottawa is the driving force of the Citizens'. It was his idea for the organization's secrecy."

"Who is he?"

"No idea."

"Bob, you aren't giving me much to report."

"I know, I know. I *can* tell you about the *Citizen*."

"What's that?"

"Their paper. It's directly under the authority of a Publicity Committee and all articles are submitted to this committee for approval. It's set here, purposely printed out of town in Selkirk, and then transported back to Winnipeg."

"Good. Any more details?"

"The paper was distributed at some local churches this morning and at all the fire stations except the one in Weston. One more thing — unlike the *Labour News*, the *Citizen* is free."

"What's it like?"

"See for yourself." Crandall smiled and handed Patterson a copy of the first issue. Patterson focused on the main editorial.

```
It must be stated that this publication
is not issued on behalf of workers, nor
employers, nor in opposition to either
of them. It is to the general public of
Winnipeg that we speak, in stating without
equivocation that this is not a strike at
all in the ordinary sense of the term —
it is plain Revolution. It is a serious
attempt to overthrow British institutions
in this Western country and to supplant
them with the Russian Bolshevik system of
Soviet rule.
```

Patterson felt Crandall's eyes boring into him as he read. "What do you think?"

Patterson put the paper down. "Looks like the gloves are off now."

"Ain't that the truth," Crandall commented, and glanced at his pocket watch. "Do you want to meet later tonight, or are you going back over the border again?"

"No," Patterson said, shaking his head side to side. "Someone else is."

"Who?"

"*You.*"

Crandall grimaced. "*Me?*"

"Mr. Anderson will pay you ten dollars a day plus expenses. All you have to do is make sure the Western Union telegrapher wires our dispatches."

"*Our* dispatches?"

"That's right. Anderson wants my stuff, some we do together and a few of your own."

"Will I get paid for the work we do together?"

"Yep, and we share the byline. Plus you will be paid the space rate for several smaller stories over your signature, so don't forget to get them wired too."

"I don't know. It's one hell of a long way . . ."

"All right. What will it take?" pleaded Patterson.

"Sweeten it to twenty bucks a day plus expenses."

"I'm in no mood to argue. You've got a deal, even if the extra ten comes out of my pocket."

"What about future dispatches?'

"Same understanding, as long as the strike persists and the local telegraphers stay off the job."

"Okay, you're on." Crandall grinned.

Chapter 21
Winnipeg
The Strike — Day 7

Tanned and fit, Mayor Charles Gray greeted Patterson with an easy smile. "You're with an Eastern newspaper."

"Yes. The *Toronto Advocate*."

"You've come a long way for a story."

"True, but the strike is newsworthy and interest is national."

Scrutinizing Patterson, Gray replied, "How can I help you?"

Patterson pulled out his notepad. "I understand you tried to avert the walkout."

"Yes."

"Can you provide an example?"

"I telephoned WTLC President James Winning the evening before the walkout began and asked him if the iron workers agreed to concede demands, would the strike be abandoned."

"What did he say?"

"He said, 'Well, it might help, but it's too late to discuss that now.' At that point and in the presence of Manitoba's Attorney General, I telegraphed the Acting Prime Minister requesting full co-operation to effect his early settlement of the dispute."

"Is there any truth to the allegations in the American press and wire services, as well as in rumours throughout the city, that municipal government has abdicated?"

From the brief flash of emotion in Gray's eyes, Patterson could tell this was a sensitive issue with the mayor. "The Union Jack," he declared, "is flying high above City Hall at this moment, and it will continue to fly there."

"Can I quote you?"

"Absolutely!"

"Also, there is a rumour that you will be deported and a full-fledged Soviet government instituted."

"That's absolutely ridiculous!"

Scribbling down the mayor's reply, Patterson continued, "The people in the East are tremendously interested in the Winnipeg strike and in manifestations of what seems to be considered by a good many citizens as Bolshevik, contrasted with ordinary, municipal rule. Are the strikers in control of the city?"

"Are you referring particularly to the issue of the Strike Committee's permit cards?"

"Yes. Can you explain this issue?"

"Certainly. It was a question of motive — why those cards were placed on certain restaurants, movie theatres, and bread, milk and ice wagons. The strikers maintain that these notices and permits were given not as a dictatorial act but as a protection afforded by the Strike Committee to certain union workers who would have been on strike had it not been considered necessary to keep the people fed."

"Who authorized the cards?"

"Mr. Carruthers, the owner of Crescent Creamery, approached City Hall as soon as the strike started for some means to deliver milk and at the same time protect his rigs and drivers. Other employers soon followed with similar requests. Following their appeals, a meeting was held to provide them with an answer, which ultimately was use of the permit cards on wagons, restaurants and theatres. In fact I was reliably informed by the Strike Committee the same employers who requested these permits personally put them up after going to the Labour Temple."

"Who attended this meeting and made the decision about the cards?"

"A number of people, including Mr. Carruthers, members of the Strike Committee, Aldermen Fisher, Sparling, Hamlin and Queen and two members of the Citizens'."

"I understand one of the Citizens' representatives was Alfred Andrews."

"Yes."

"As a Citizens' member, former mayor and lawyer, I imagine he played a significant role in the discussion of the strike cards."

"Mr. Patterson, both Andrews and his colleague made it quite clear their attendance at the meeting was in the capacity of private citizens."

"Interesting." Patterson paused to write down his answer. "Though everyone knows they're Citizens' members."

"That's open to interpretation."

"So approving the cards was really a collaborative decision?"

"Of course," answered Gray.

"And not one made unilaterally by the Strike Committee, as various American and Canadian news reports are claiming?"

"That's correct."

"There is another development I hope you can clarify."

Gray shifted uneasily. "Which development?"

"A major issue in the strike is union recognition."

"Yes."

"I have been told representatives of the three companies being struck by metal-trades workers have informed you they'll no longer negotiate with striking employees until they return to work."

"That's true."

"It seems strange that these employers would not encourage unions and their recognition."

When Gray did not respond, Patterson added, "I also understand their decision was dictated by the Citizens'."

"Yes."

"What is your reaction to this?"

Gray hesitated. Before he could answer, there was a knock on the door.

A city official entered. "Sorry to interrupt, Your Worship, but a matter needs your immediate attention."

Gray stood and extended a hand to Patterson. "That's all the time I have now."

Patterson bit his tongue. He had further questions, but they would have to wait. He shook Gray's hand. "Thank you for your time."

He had to dig deeper. It was becoming apparent the Citizens' was influencing, if not controlling, the strike's outcome. Also, despite the anti-strike organization's claim the walkout was a Bolshevik-inspired attempt to overturn constituted authority and replace it with a Soviet-style government, Patterson had not yet found a shred of evidence to support the theory.

He needed answers.

By the time he reached the Alex, he knew who to ask.

Chapter 22
Winnipeg
The Strike — Day 7

Patterson found Crandall in the Criterion drinking with a *Trib* reporter. When Crandall waved Patterson over, the reporter quickly finished his drink and left. "You look frustrated," said Crandall. "Want a drink?"

"No," exclaimed Patterson. "You've been playing me!"

Crandall's face turned serious. "What do you mean?"

"You know what I mean!"

"All right, all right. What do you want?"

"I want answers. I want the truth."

"Ask away."

"Will the strikers win?"

"Not a chance. Moose will be flying before that happens."

"Why didn't you tell me this the first time? You withheld information that would've helped me report this story accurately and fairly from the start. You led me to believe reds were behind the strike. The Citizens' paper is claiming the strike is 'plain ugly revolution' and the wire services are reporting Bolsheviks are in control and armed reds lurking behind every corner. But I've my doubts now that any of this is true."

"Look, I'm sorry, but —"

Patterson cut him off. "Both of us know there's a big difference between suspicion of and actual subversive activity."

Sidestepping Patterson's remark, Crandall looked at him squarely. "Do you know what happened on the West Coast last February? A massive general sympathetic strike erupted in Seattle, but the city's mayor, Ole Hanson, quickly persuaded the public the whole thing was a red conspiracy. Despite facing 60,000 strikers, Hanson deputized thousands of special police, threatened to bring in the military and crushed the walkout."

"Are you telling me same thing will happen here?"

"Not as fast, but here's my prediction. The local authorities and the business community will play the Bolshevik card and the majority on City Council will claim the strike is Soviet-style revolution. Premier Norris will conveniently sit on the sidelines for a while and then find a way to get the telephone exchanges operating again, and the federal government will force reinstatement of mail service. Meanwhile, the owners of Manitoba Bridge, Vulcan and Dominion Bridge will follow the dictates of the Citizens' and ignore the strikers' demand for union recognition and better wages until the men return to work."

"Anything else?"

"The local press will crucify the strike and its leaders, and once the people who really wield power in the city as if it is a birthright get organized, they'll force the authorities to arrest those in charge and either toss them into Stony Mountain Penitentiary or some godforsaken camp in Kapuskasing. Perhaps they can even have the strike leaders deported."

"Could the strike get violent?"

"Ivens and the Strike Committee say no, and the police union is taking orders from the Labour Temple to stay on the job, so it appears not. However, if the police are fired and replaced by men unacceptable to the Strike Committee, or if martial law is declared and Ketchen brings in the militia, then there really could be bloodshed. Also, no one knows for sure which side the retuned men will take."

"Which side do you think they'll support?"

"Even though the veterans' associations have adopted a policy of neutrality in the strike, the majority will support the walkout. On the other hand, a lot of these guys are mad as hell about not being able to find work, and they blame enemy aliens — you know, foreigners in the North End — for taking their jobs. Also, even though the Spanish flu has tapered off, it has killed over 1,200 people here and there's a lot of resentment towards immigrant families for spreading the disease. So there could be big trouble against strikers by demobilized men if they believe Slavs and Jews caused the death of so many residents *and* the strike leaders are mixed up with Bolshevik foreigners. Everyone knows the returned men used rifles and bullets to settle things in the trenches, so there's fear they could turn the city into another battlefield."

"Why didn't you tell me these things earlier?"

"I apologize. You're a good guy, Patterson, well-intentioned but naive. You want the truth, well here it is. The strikers are in a knife fight without a knife, and no one is going to support their side of the story instead of the Citizens'."

"Why?"

"Don't you understand? The men in the Citizens' have power, position and prestige, not to mention unlimited resources. You would think Ivens, Russell and company would've learned by now not to kick a lion in the arse if you can't deal with his teeth."

Patterson grew silent.

"Look, kid, here's some free advice. Reporting is not a business for a nice young man. It's a tough, hard business and it's dirty too. You work hard and you work long and you never make any money. You don't get to live as other people do. You get to know things that are better unknown. You grow old and tired and sad on the job and wake up wondering what the hell happened to you."

Crandall finished his drink, stood and left. But not before handing Patterson a note. He waited until Crandall had gone to read it.

Senator Robertson is on his way to Winnipeg, accompanied by Arthur Meighen. Two Citizens' executive members will intercept them in Fort William and persuade them to end the strike by any means, including force. Alfred Andrews may be one of the Citizens' members. Hope this information makes amends.

Patterson stared at his empty glass. *If Crandall is right and the strike is a lost cause, should I give up on the story now? Or should I become personally involved?* One thing was certain — the more he learned, the more he needed to know. The hunt for the truth was just beginning.

Chapter 23
Fort William
May 22, 1919

Senator Robertson and Minister of Justice Arthur Meighen waited in the Labour Minister's private CPR railway car for two visitors, both lawyers, from the Citizens'. The two cabinet members sat quietly, both deep in thought, saving conversation for the secret meeting.

In the absence of reliable information from Winnipeg, Robertson was following the strike in the press and wire services. Early news reports described Winnipeg as *the epicenter of revolution* and *a Bolshevik assault on constituted authority*. The *New York Times* headlined the strike *Leninism in Winnipeg*, and the *Chicago Tribune* characterized it as *A Red Plan* and *Industrial Revolution*. Robertson had also been informed by foreign affairs officials there was pressure from the United States government to intervene in the dispute, due to the Red Scare.

Robertson knew there were several complications involving the strike. First, if it disrupted railway traffic, the effects on the Canadian economy would be disastrous. Second, given recent events in Russia and the spread of Bolshevism, class warfare had erupted in several countries. Unfortunately, a similar situation seemed to be developing in Winnipeg. Finally, there were the returned soldiers. Over 15,000 demobilized men were in Winnipeg and hundreds were arriving weekly. While the officers would likely oppose the mass tie-up, the majority of enlisted men might support it. The inherent danger of so many battle-hardened and unemployed men in the strike's charged atmosphere deeply troubled Robertson.

A knock on the door interrupted his thoughts. "Sorry to disturb you, Senator," announced the conductor, "but the men you're expecting have arrived on the through train."

"Thank you," Robertson responded.

When the two well-dressed men arrived, he said, "Gentlemen, please come in. I presume you know the Minister of Justice."

"We've met before. Good evening, Mr. Meighen."

"Good evening," Meighen replied.

As Robertson retrieved several thick files from his briefcase, Meighen and the two visitors sat down at a table. Joining them, Robertson invited conversation to begin.

The older, clearly the lead, spoke first. "Thank you for seeing us. The Citizens' believes the strikers' goal is the overthrow of the city's constitutionally elected government and therefore an attack on law and order and the citizens of Winnipeg."

Robertson turned to the younger lawyer. "Do you agree?"

"Indeed. Bolshevism has reared its ugly head in Winnipeg and must be quickly stamped out. We need your help to deal with the strike leaders."

"What about the rank-and-file union members?"

"The majority of those on strike are extremely naive but nevertheless dangerous because they've been stampeded into action by leaders with false promises," stated the lead.

"What proof do you have of your allegations?"

"The strike leaders have said as much in public meetings and in their paper, which is now being circulated freely in the city. They've become the de facto government of Winnipeg, and despite what Mayor Gray is telling the press, it's a miracle the Union Jack is still flying over City Hall. These reds have control of essential public services and are threatening the city with financial ruin."

"What do you want from us?"

"Given complete industrial and political revolution by these Bolshevik strike leaders, can't you arrest and deport them?"

"It's not that simple," interjected Meighen. "Most are Anglo-Saxon and almost all are British immigrants. Yet, if sedition can be proven, I may consider setting aside some constitutional restraints, even for British subjects."

"What about the non-union supporters, many of whom are registered alien enemies?" the younger lawyer interjected.

"For immigrants there are fewer legal entanglements," Meighen assured. "Internment and deportation would be better than prosecution in the courts. However, it appears there are no foreigners in the strike's leadership."

"Can't anything be done about these British-born radicals?"

"Perhaps there is some way to amend the Immigration Act and remove their immunity from deportation. What I need is a special representative of the Ministry of Justice in Winnipeg to ascertain if this strike is an attempt to usurp the powers of the duly elected representatives of the people."

Both visitors remained silent.

Looking at the lead, Meighen said, "Would you accept this appointment?"

"Indeed I would."

"Thank you."

At this point Robertson interrupted. "Gentlemen, I concur it's time to act. Your opinions support my own belief — this sympathetic strike is a cloak for something far deeper than legitimate labour demands. The government of Canada will not allow union radicals to dictate to the law-abiding citizens of Winnipeg. I'll persuade the city's postal workers to return to their jobs, or they'll lose them, and I'll have little sympathy to grant these men employment again in the federal government should they not comply with the conditions of reinstatement."

He waited for the effect of his pronouncement.

A relieved look passed between the two visitors. "On behalf of the Citizens', thank you," they responded. "These strikers must be taught a lesson."

"Yes," confirmed Robertson. "Now, let me share some information gathered by our national intelligence apparatus on Bolsheviks, Socialists and Enemy Aliens. What you're about to read is of a highly sensitive nature and knowledge of this material must remain confidential."

"We understand."

"Good. Then, gentlemen, let's begin."

Chapter 24
Winnipeg
The Strike — Day 8

Hearing that able-bodied volunteers were needed to replace striking firemen, Bear offered his services to the Citizens'.

"I want to help because it's the right thing to do," he lied, "and because people's lives and property will be in danger without fire service." When asked if he felt it was his civic duty to volunteer, he nodded. "Yes. I was in the army and know how important duty is." It wasn't really a lie. He would be helping people in need, abandoned by those who were supposed to protect them — so what if it might gain him their job after the strike was over. He was a loyal citizen who deserved the employment.

Given his eagerness, muscular appearance and returned-soldier status, Bear was quickly recruited and sent to the main fire station on Albert Street. Once there, he started to feel better, but the feeling didn't last.

The city had almost 400 street call boxes, and strikers kept volunteer firefighters busy day and night by continually setting off false alarms at several of the boxes. Worse still was the reception firefighters received when they answered a call. They arrived to find a fake fire and a large and hostile crowd of strikers taunting them with shouts of *rotten scabs* and *yellow strikebreakers*.

During his third day on the job, Bear and his fellow fire-fighters were called to a real fire at the Auditorium. By the time they arrived and set up fire-fighting equipment, the familiar landmark was ablaze and smoke was billowing out all sides of the building. The captain told Bear to handle one of the big hoses at the front of the building, and for several minutes the flow enabled him to send a steady stream into the blaze.

Suddenly it dropped to a trickle.

Bear yelled for more pressure but nothing happened. Wondering if there was something wrong with the coupler, he ran back to the hydrant only to find someone had deliberately cut the hose.

Across the street half a dozen flat-capped men were watching, saying nothing but pointing at him and laughing. Then one of the men held up an axe and smiled. Bear snapped. Not caring he was outnumbered, he dropped the heavy hose and, roaring like a wounded animal, charged across the street.

The strikers were slow to react to Bear's sudden action, and before they knew it he'd kicked one between the legs and levelled another with a quick uppercut and jab to the head. Turning to face the next man, Bear caught a vicious punch to the jaw. The blow shot needles through his face, but he managed to elbow the attacker in the solar plexus. By this time Bear's fellow firemen were racing across the street to help even the odds. Seeing the firefighters coming, the rest of the strikers scattered, leaving one of their comrades on the ground. Bear straddled the moaning striker and glared down at him. "Now you're going to pay, you Bolshevik bastard," he howled, and repeatedly kicked him in the ribs, the blows making sickening cracking sounds.

It took four firefighters to pull Bear off the bruised and battered man. As he returned to the fire, Bear rubbed his jaw and tasted blood inside his mouth. Though the whole left side of his face throbbed painfully, for the first time in months he felt good.

"What happened?" demanded the captain.

"One of those red bastards cut the hose with an axe."

"Why did you go alone? You could've been beaten up pretty badly. Our job is to put out fires, not get into scraps."

Bear faked an apologetic expression. "I know. I'm sorry." What he didn't reveal was the fight was his first step in getting justice for Jenny and Michael.

Chapter 25
Winnipeg
The Strike – Day 9

*T*wo *Citizens' executive members will intercept the ministers . . . to end the strike by any means, including force.*

What did Crandall mean?

Patterson strode down the street, barely looking where he was going. He had learned from Mayor Gray that the Citizens' were blocking a settlement of the strike between the metal-trades workers and their employers. Was the same organization also now conspiring with the government?

He thought he knew a good place to find answers — the Industrial Bureau.

He found the barn-like structure, with its long row of flags and pointed dome topped by an enormous Union Jack, at the corner of Main and Water Streets. In front of the building a steady stream of automobiles, jitneys, motorcycles and bicycles was coming and going, seemingly scouting up and down Main and Portage. Several Fords, Packards and McLaughlins were turned in against the curb with noses angled to the sidewalks, reminding Patterson of ships moored to a dock.

There was no doubt the cavernous structure was the Citizens' command post, because over the double doors of the front entrance hung a sign with large black lettering proclaiming THE HEAD-QUARTERS CITIZENS' COMMITTEE OF ONE THOUSAND. Outside the building were several well-dressed men sporting small Union Jacks in their coat lapels, a symbol Patterson knew had been adopted by those opposed to the strike.

Passing through the double-door entrance, he encountered a uniformed soldier signing up fire and telephone-operator volunteers, but before he could question the veteran, two men — one short and squat, the other tall and angular — intercepted him. They had their muscular arms crossed, and under their blazers he could see the bulge of holstered revolvers.

"Are you here to volunteer?" asked the tall one.

"Not really."

"What the hell do you want, then?" shot his partner.

"To go in."

Shaking his head from side to side, the tall one said, "Only bona fide Citizens' members are permitted inside."

Opening his wallet, Patterson removed his *Advocate* press badge. Showing it to them, he said, "I'm a reporter."

They looked at each other and checked the identification. "Wait here," remarked the tall one, and went inside. Meanwhile, his partner just glared.

Patterson attempted to make conversation but was quickly cut off. "Save your breath. We don't let the local press in, so being an outsider, you're really shit out of luck."

"All right, but if you don't mind, I'll wait."

"Suit yourself."

A few minutes later a man in his forties emerged. He had swept-back greying hair, hard blue eyes, tobacco-stained teeth and a face like a bulldog.

"I'm with the *Toronto Advocate*," Patterson announced, and offered his hand.

The man ignored the gesture. His eyes conveyed his thoughts loud and clear: *I've got nothing to say to you.*

Patterson bluffed. "I'm here on official business."

"We aren't allowing reporters inside!" came the gruff reply.

Patterson is thrown out of the Citizens' headquarters.

"I need to speak to the Citizens' members who met the Minsters of Labour and Justice in Fort William last night."

Sensing the man's hesitation, Patterson improvised. "I just have a few questions. It won't take long."

The man shook his head. "I don't know who you're talking about and already said *no press*. Now, unless you want my two friends here to escort you onto the street, I strongly suggest you leave."

Before Paterson could answer, the man spun around and left him facing the two menacing doormen. They dropped their arms, clenched their fists and scowled. "You heard him. Now piss off!"

"I'm not going anywhere," Patterson insisted, and braced himself. The punch in the stomach doubled him over. Then both of his arms were pinned and he was tossed onto the sidewalk. Landing hard, he looked up to see if more pain was coming, but his attackers were gone.

Chapter 25
Winnipeg
The Strike — Day 9

Patterson picked up a copy of the *Labour News* on his way back to the Alex. There, he learned that Mayor Gray had invited representatives from the railway unions, Strike Committee, Citizens' Committee and City Council to discuss an end to the strike. The public meeting was to be held in City Hall's Council Chamber starting at 9:00 p.m. He quickly changed course.

While he waited in the Council Chamber for the meeting to begin, Patterson continued to peruse the paper. Robertson had arrived in Winnipeg, the strikers' food kitchen — the Labour Café — had opened at the Strathcona Hotel, department stores had resumed deliveries, gas stations had reopened, the *Free Press* had republished and over 6,000 strikers and returned men had attended an open-air meeting at Victoria Park. Neither side was giving ground. *The longer this goes on, the more difficult it will be to resolve.*

A tired-looking Mayor Gray entered the room and sat at the head of the Chamber's round, dark wood table. At precisely nine o'clock he banged his gavel to start proceedings. As Gray began his introductory remarks, Patterson removed his notepad. A few rows over, a red-faced and heavily sweating man wearing a rumpled suit and chomping on a frayed cigar did the same.

They made eye contact. He nodded at Patterson.

The discussion opened on the contentious issue of collective bargaining, with a railway official systematically explaining how seven different metal trades on the railways already bargained together with fourteen different railways. He finished by stating the current general strike was started with a view to enforcing similar collective bargaining in the contract metal shops.

After several minutes on this topic, Alfred Andrews and Bob Russell entered the discussion. Old enough to be Russell's father, Andrews had tousled iron-grey hair, long in the front and thin, and a clean-shaven face. Patterson leaned forward in his seat. He was determined not to miss anything Andrews said.

"The discussion so far has been very enlightening to me," Andrews began. "Our object here is solution of a pressing problem. I'm satisfied there'll be no negotiations, and the strike will break unless the postal clerks go back, the firemen resume work and the policemen are well rooted in their positions. It would be splendid diplomacy if you give assurances along that line before there are further defections from your ranks."

"What's your idea?" challenged Russell.

"A number of sympathetic strikers are returning to their jobs. At nine o'clock Monday morning, the government re-starts the postal service. There is no trouble getting men. It has been demonstrated that volunteers can fight fires and public services are going to be run. Business has been affected to some extent. You can say the strike will be extended from ocean to ocean, but the rights of the citizens will be associated in every part of the Dominion. You must get your rights in some other way. I'm the real friend of every man present. A limited telephone service is now being given. Monday the postal men will be shut out. They went out in sympathy and will lose their seniority. Telephone girls have come to me crying. It's not necessary to get a definition of collective bargaining. That is going to be given to you. But when a man breaks into my garage and steals my car and gets into my house and takes my furniture, I'm not going to bargain with him, until he makes redress."

"We haven't broken into your house or stolen your car."

"No, but you made the firemen, to whom we trust our life, break the agreement not to strike before May 1920, almost before the ink was dry," retorted Andrews.

"Made them?" Russell fired back.

"Well, permitted them," replied Andrews smoothly, "and I would lose everything I have rather than bargain with you before they return. Remember, you never lose anything by doing what is good. You have a dream that is something to realize — not collective bargaining merely — but the control of society by your organization. It may come someday, but the sooner you reestablish the public services here and everywhere, the better. Public opinion is against you."

Russell cleared his throat. "I hope you give us credit for understanding the basis of society. The feudal system is going out. Who is the citizen to whom you say we should restore his rights? You say you are representing the citizens. But there are 35,000 strikers and if there is an average of three dependents on each, that makes 105,000 out of a population of less than 200,000. The workmen in their economic organizations say they are the producers of wealth. Withdraw labour and no more wealth is produced, as we have proved. Hasn't the workingman the right to demand from you the proportion of wealth that he creates? We haven't defied authority, but have recognized it from start to finish. Never from the start have our tactics been an attack on the state."

At this point Mayor Gray and two aldermen, followed by the railway representatives, took over the discussion. The meeting continued for several hours, with no further exchanges between Andrews and Russell and with no resolution in sight.

Towards midnight a clearly frustrated and impatient Andrews made a final statement. "Every sane man changes his opinions but it's my firm determination and I may as well withdraw as being of no further service, unless the firemen are to go back, and a pledge be given not to call sympathetic strikes of public utility workers before we discuss a settlement. This is final. Your methods are wrong and we will not endorse them. You should be manly enough to say you made a mistake." Upon finishing, he stared at Russell, collected his notes and stood.

Mayor Gray cleared his throat loudly. "Gentlemen, when should the next meeting be held?" There was no response, only silence. Gray wearily rubbed his fingertips over tired eyes. "In that case, please be aware that I'll be in my office at any time to assist in negotiations."

As the Council Chamber emptied, Patterson flipped through his notes. They were more than ample. Particularly important were the exchanges between Andrews and Russell. Both were like well-trained and well-matched boxers, exchanging blows but no knock-out punches and no blood — yet.

It was midnight. He stood, stretched and yawned.

Chapter 27
Winnipeg
The Strike — Day 9

The rotund note-taking man who had nodded at Patterson before the meeting began was approaching. In a hoarse voice, he stated, "Some shooting match, wasn't it? Like an old-fashioned Wild West show, complete with gunslingers."

"I would say a lot of talk but, sadly, little concrete results. More of a standoff than a shootout," Patterson replied matter-of-factly.

"Well, in this town you soon learn that bulldogs outnumber lapdogs."

Patterson arched an eyebrow.

"May I present myself, sir. My name is Colonel Graham H. Davies," the bespectacled old-timer announced with a Dixie drawl. Running a hand across a sweaty scalp, he handed Patterson a card with an address embossed in copperplate script. Printed in bold letters was *Davies International Press News Bureau. Royal Alexandra Hotel. Winnipeg.*

Patterson scanned the card and looked up. Davies was short, stout and red-faced, with hard little blue eyes. He wore a neatly parted toupee which didn't match his greying red hair and sat like a daub of paint on his round head. Patterson guessed he was nudging sixty pretty hard, and from the gin blossoms over his nose and on his cheeks and the bulge of the pocket-flask in his suit coat, a heavy drinker.

Davies pointed at Patterson's notepad. "I'd say you are either a reporter or an RNWMP agent" (referring to the Royal North-West Mounted Police).

"I'm with the *Toronto Advocate*."

"The *Advocate*," Davies repeated and frowned. "Your paper must want this story pretty badly to send you halfway across the country."

"My paper wants the truth," Patterson corrected.

Davies laughed mirthlessly. "The truth, if you *really* want it, is that these godforsaken strikers are scheming reds who want a program of Soviet rule. This so-called strike has all the fingerprints of revolution. An industrial siege is happening here, and without men like Alfred Andrews we would be hopeless and helpless. In my opinion we should be arresting and deporting any Bolshevik who dares show his face in Winnipeg. For God's sake, can't you see we're becoming the damned Petrograd of Canada?"

"What about the foreigners?" Patterson questioned. "I'm told there is not a single one in the strike leadership."

"Haven't you read Kipling?" Davies bristled. "'A man should, whatever happens, keep to his own caste, race and breed.' There are more than 27,000 registered enemy aliens in Winnipeg, from Germany, Austria, Hungary, the Ottoman Empire and Bulgaria, just waiting to cause trouble."

"Where are they?"

"In the North End, where else? Hebes, Bohunks, Pukes and Polacks — and every last one has little or no loyalty to this country. They're backward. They're peasants. They're ignorant. They're not like us. And they've spread the Spanish flu." Almost winded from his rant, Davies caught his breath. "For all we know, Bolshevik-led revolutionaries have dynamite and arms secretly stockpiled and are already drilling. Doesn't that scare you?"

Before Patterson could answer, Davies winked and lowered his voice. "Since the strike began I've kept a loaded pistol in my desk at the Royal Alex and carry it wherever I go." He opened his hand and revealed, then re-pocketed, a silver-plated derringer. "In my younger days I could shoot the spots off a playing card at twenty feet with this little beauty."

"Are you a newspaperman or a private detective?" Patterson asked.

"A newspaperman. Moved from Kentucky to your fair Dominion in '97, after the authorities south of the border took too much of an interest in me following a duel I won. Did a little reporting for the *Toronto World*, and after this tried my luck as a Klondike prospector and stampeder. Made it to Dawson City by way of the Chilkoot in late '98, but never struck it rich. After that I spent some time with the *Calgary Eye-Opener* on the rewrite and copy editor's desks, and moved to Winnipeg in 1906, where I joined the *Telegram*. For ten years I was the paper's editor, but recently I struck out on my own and started a press service."

"Why?"

"Simple. When I became the *Tely*'s editor I quickly learned two things. First, I couldn't do the reporting for my reporters and I had to trust them. Second, I hated trusting anybody, so after one too many screaming matches in the newsroom I decided to report for myself. Now I freelance for several British and American papers and the big wire services, as well as stringing for Canadian dailies. When customers are willing to pay, I'm their man."

Moving a little closer, Davies confided, "Seeing that we're now both part of the newspaper fraternity and you're a stranger in town, I'll be happy to help you out, if you know what I mean."

"How?" replied Patterson cautiously.

"You scratch my back and I'll scratch yours, that's how. Since the local press, American news hawks and yours truly are persona non grata with the Strike Committee, and because your paper is labour-friendly, it'll be easy for you to get into the Labour Temple and talk to guys like Russell, who after tonight's performance, you can see makes for good copy."

When Patterson said nothing, Davies added, "You can be our insider."

"*Our* insider?"

"Yes. After you give me information, I can do a little quid pro quo."

"What can you give me?"

"I know the local and provincial government officials and most of the executive members of the Citizens'. They've dealt with me before and are familiar with how I work, so why don't we give-and-take information from our separate pipelines."

"How are you going to get the executive members to talk?"

"We horse trade. I get reliable inside information in a timely fashion, and in return the organization gets its side of events printed and well treated in my stories. Sometimes it costs me a few bucks, but that's life."

Davies was clearly both crafty and shrewd. Patterson had to admit the offer was tempting.

"Forget it!" said Patterson. "I don't believe in paying my sources or printing their opinions as fact, and I don't do puff pieces. I'm a reporter, not a hired gun."

Davies threw his head back and laughed out loud. "Hired gun! That's rich, Patterson, but I prefer to see myself as an interpreter and enlivener of events. It may not be ethical journalism, but it helps me make a living." Letting his words sink in, Davies paused, then eyed Patterson challengingly. "You wouldn't be so self-righteous, nor would your Simon-pure publisher Anderson, about how a story was obtained if you could get a heart-stopping front page scoop, right?"

Before Patterson could answer, Davies pulled out a watch on a gold chain, theatrically checked the time and said breezily, "Think it over, Mr. Patterson. I'm in Room 307. Now it's time for me to write up this story and get it on the wire."

"Before you go," said Patterson, "tell me something. I don't yet completely understand why the local dailies and American reporters are crusading against the strike and its leaders."

"It's really quite simple. The strike leaders are reds and the rank and file are Bolshevik sympathizers, so they're getting the press coverage they damn well deserve."

With that Davies stood up to leave. "Much obliged to meet you, Mr. Patterson." Tipping his homburg, Davies ambled out of the Council Chamber in a lazy shuffle and disappeared down the corridor.

Chapter 28
Winnipeg
The Strike — Day 10

Patterson waited outside the main post office on Smith Street, tapping his foot against the pavement. Senator Robertson had summoned all striking postal employees there at noon to hear an ultimatum.

Something important was about to happen.

Promptly at noon and accompanied by an armed bodyguard, Robertson arrived at the post office in a black McLaughlin. He was greeted outside the building by the postmaster.

Patterson lingered within earshot.

"Good afternoon, Senator Robertson. There's been some unexpected trouble here," announced the postmaster.

"What do you mean?"

"The men have been redirected by the Strike Committee to the Labour Temple instead of coming to your meeting. There are less than 75 of 300 postal employees waiting inside."

Robertson frowned. "I will make the announcement anyway," he insisted, and strode past him, but before he reached the front entrance, the postmaster stopped him.

"There's another problem."

"What?"

"Bob Russell is at the front door. He's been there for over an hour, persuading the men to go to the Labour Temple. Senator, I warn you, he's in a feisty mood."

"What arrogance!" exclaimed Robertson. "As I don't wish to confront *that* man, we'll go in the back door."

"Well, sir, that's also a problem."

"*Why?*" a now completely exasperated Robertson snapped.

Patterson listens to Robertson's announcement at the post office.

"Reverend William Ivens is at the back door."

"Out of my way!" Robertson bristled as he marched defiantly towards the front entrance. "We're going in. Russell or not."

As Robertson and his bodyguard approached the front door, Russell breezily greeted Robertson. "Good afternoon, Senator. Welcome to Winnipeg."

"Good day to you, sir," Robertson shot back, and brushed by the grinning strike leader.

The postmaster led Robertson and his bodyguard into the post office's cavernous sorting room, where dozens of men were waiting.

Patterson slipped into the crowd.

Robertson wasted no time in pleasantries. "Men, the postal service has been denied to the citizens of Winnipeg since May 15. This has been done at the dictation of a small body of men not connected with the postal organization. The employees sworn to faithfully serve the State in their several capacities have deserted that service. They have done so entirely without reference to any grievance of their own and, indeed, within a few weeks of an adjustment acknowledged by themselves to be satisfactory. Under these conditions, they have chosen, without notice and on a sympathetic issue, to dislocate and paralyze the public service of a great community."

He paused, waiting for his words to take effect. "Starting tomorrow voluntary workers will be temporarily taking the jobs postal employees have left. Furthermore, the government of Canada announces those returning before twelve o'clock noon of Monday, May 26 will be accepted, and all failing to resume their duties by that hour will be definitely refused thereafter a place in the federal service. Commencing at the above-stated hour, new employees will be engaged on the usual permanent basis."

When finished, Robertson looked gravely at the men. "I cannot overemphasize the federal government's commitment in returning postal service to the citizens of Winnipeg. You should also be aware that each employee who returns to work on Monday morning will be required to sign a pledge never to strike in sympathy again and to break all membership ties with the WTLC."

"The pledge is nothing but a slave pact!" blurted someone in front of Patterson.

Robertson ignored the comment.

"What about our pensions?" asked an older man.

"Failure to comply with every reinstatement condition will result in all pension benefits and rights being forfeited," responded Robertson. With that he turned and, with his bodyguard leading the way, left the building.

Patterson recorded Robertson's parting remarks and waited until he had gone before racing back to the Alex for an interview.

He intercepted Robertson in the lobby. "Senator Robertson, may I please have a minute?"

"Mr. Patterson. I'm rather busy."

"Just two questions."

"All right."

"First, do you intend to enforce the ultimatum on postal employees?"

"Certainly, though I hope they'll return to work before the deadline and avoid the consequences."

"Second, both you and Minister of Justice Meighen have been quoted in today's *Citizen* issue as regarding the Winnipeg general strike as 'a cloak for something far deeper — a cloak to overturn proper authority.' Do you both stand by this statement?"

"Yes."

"Are you suggesting the strike has an ulterior motive in the form of a Soviet plot?"

"I am indeed."

Chapter 29
Toronto
May 26, 1919

Joseph Anderson read the final proofs of Patterson's strike news before the copy went to press for the evening edition. In 72-point black letters, the paper's banner headline blared *Federal Ministers Condemn Winnipeg Strike*.

The story was placed on the front page in columns two and three, and the remainder carried over to page two. The 500-word report was drop-lined *Robertson and Meighen Declare No Justification for Walkout*. Columns one and four provided sidebar stories. The top of column five featured a head-and-shoulders picture of a white-collared *Reverend Mr. Ivens*. To complete the coverage, column six supplied Patterson's interview with Robertson.

A knock on the door interrupted Anderson. "You wanted to see me?" asked the news editor.

"Yes. Please read Patterson's dispatch. While I believe he has reported the strike situation correctly and has cast doubt on the Soviet-plot allegation by Robertson and Meighen, I want to know if you agree with his analysis. I also want your suggestions for the story's drop heads."

"Certainly, Mr. Anderson."

Special to The Advocate by William Patterson
Copyright 1919, by The Toronto Advocate
Noyes, Minnesota, May 26
(By train from Winnipeg)

With the statements of Senator Robertson, Minister of Labour, and Hon. Arthur Meighen to the effect that they regarded the Winnipeg general strike as a cloak for something deeper — a cloak for an effort to "overturn proper authority" — the question of whether or not the strike here really has an ulterior motive in the form of a Soviet plot becomes a dominant issue once again.

Not only is the right or wrong of this matter of fundamental importance, but the mere fact that the "plot" idea is held, not only by private citizens, but by responsible Ministers of the Crown both federally and provincially is a most important factor in the situation. Whether their view actually is well-founded or not, they believe it is, and their belief had coloured their actions. It has led them to come out definitely against the strike. They are not preserving neutrality, they are openly opposed to it.

Distinct from the workmen, there are those who believe that if any revolution was attempted in Winnipeg it was political rather than industrial. In reality, was it? And was it any sort of revolution at all, or merely a more or less unrealized and unappreciated rise of the private worker? When the smoke has cleared away, what may be discovered is this. A very large number of trade unionists, probably the vast majority struck on the simple and specific

issue of collective bargaining, which they
thought was being assailed in such a challenging way that there was no recourse but
to clear the issue once for all.

Senator Robertson has issued an ultimatum to striking postal employees to return to work by noon on Monday May 26 or
face dismissal and forfeit all pension
rights. Each employee who returns will be
required to sign a pledge never to strike
in sympathy again and break all membership
ties with the WTLC. All new employees will
be engaged on a permanent basis.

The editor nodded approval. "The lead is strong and I see no problems with the rest. Given the present situation in Winnipeg, Patterson's observations are relevant and discerning. For drop heads I suggest *Only a Small Proportion of the Strikers Had Revolutionary Ideas* and *Most of Them Out to Elevate Industry.*"

"Do you think we should keep him in Winnipeg?"

The editor thought for a few moments. Though not by nature a generous person, from experience he knew most new reporters were a boiling mix of self-confidence and insecurity. "His reporting is good enough, but that's not why he should stay on the story."

"Why, then?"

"Two reasons. First, Patterson knows that to stay on the story he needs to get results."

"And second?"

"He's hungry."

"Good. Run it over his byline again."

Chapter 30
Winnipeg
The Strike — Day 13

When Bob Russell entered Ivens's office in the Labour Temple, he noticed the minister's shirtsleeves were rolled up to the elbows and he was wearing his collar. While Russell had no use for religion, Ivens's life was his black leather-bound Bible and the ministry. Russell liked to tell the story about when he teased Ivens in front of a large crowd of union workers by calling the big three metal-shop owners the Holy Trinity. To his credit Ivens had graciously accepted the jibe.

The *Citizen* and local press proclaimed Ivens *the self-appointed dictator of Winnipeg*, but Russell knew the *Labour News* editor vehemently opposed violence and worked tirelessly in "His name" to champion workers' rights. *Just eat, sleep, love, laugh and look at the sun,* he had written early in the strike. *For the present in a lawful, orderly and perfectly constitutional way — do nothing.*

"Hello, friend," Russell greeted him.

"Good afternoon, Bob. I'm working on the front page for tomorrow's paper."

"May I have a look?"

Ivens handed the copy to Russell. He began to read it aloud, starting with the heading, which spanned two columns centred in the middle of the page: *What We Want and What We Don't Want.*

Under the first column Ivens had listed *the right of collective bargaining, the right to a living wage* and *the reinstatement of all strikers.* Under the latter was *Revolution, Dictatorship* and *Disorder.*

"And here's tomorrow's take on the lack of progress in settling the dispute."

> *Senator Robertson — I can do nothing till the posties return to work.*
> *Premier Norris — I can do nothing till you call off the sympathetic strike.*
> *City Council — We can do nothing till the civic employees return.*
> *Board of Trade — We can do nothing till you all go back.*
> *The Strikers — (Discordant voice) We can do nothing till you all come forward.*

"Well, there you go again," needled Russell. "I'm not one for accusations, but I believe you may be a wild-eyed revolutionary Bolshie."

"I see you've been reading the local papers," Ivens joked.

Russell's eyes twisted into an angry expression. "They're lying sons of —"

"I can also see, as usual, you're in a fighting mood," interrupted Ivens, and changed the subject. "Speaking of the press, reporter William Patterson from the *Toronto Advocate* is going to be here shortly for an interview. I think he can help our cause."

"How?"

"The *Advocate* is giving the strike front-page news coverage and is editorially sympathetic to our side. In fact the paper may be the *only* major Canadian newspaper giving us fair coverage and backing."

"Can this guy be trusted?"

"Yes. I believe he'll report our side more truthfully than any other newspaperman or wire service correspondent."

"Why?"

"He's a straight guy, a reporter, period, not a columnist. Plus the *Advocate* supports the workingman. Regardless, he'll ask you some pretty direct questions, so give him straight answers. I know you don't trust reporters, Bob, but we have few friends in the press."

"I'll talk to him," agreed Russell, "but then I've got to go, because things are really heating up. Manitoba Telephones is back operating, pro-strike vets are meeting tonight, and the city has given the police the same ultimatum Robertson gave the postal workers."

"What *is* the situation with the police?"

"Nothing has changed. The men are on the job, but I'm willing to bet the Police Commission will soon fire them and even replace MacPherson. When that happens, there'll be trouble."

There was a knock on the door — a single rap. A young man in a grey three-piece suit stood in the doorway, looking polite but determined. Ivens invited Patterson in and introduced him to Russell. They shook hands.

"I know how busy you are, Mr. Russell, so thank you for agreeing to an interview."

"Frankly, Mr. Patterson, you're one of the very few members of the press we've allowed into our headquarters since the strike began. We hope your paper will continue to provide fair coverage."

"The *Advocate* has always supported labour," countered Patterson, "and if Winnipeg workers' demands are legitimate and employers are refusing to acknowledge them, our paper wants to help readers understand why."

Russell studied Patterson. The other man's eyes were steady and honest.

What the hell, he can't do any more damage than the other papers have already. "Are you aware municipal, provincial and federal governments, as well as the Citizens' and the press, have lined up against the strike?" declared Russell.

"That remains to be proven, doesn't it?"

"Nevertheless, I would call their action a courtship with the devil. When Robertson arrived a few days ago, he met those opposed to the strike but told us 'it would not be consistent with the dignity of a Minister of the Crown to attend the Strike Committee.' Seems shameful a former union man is using bullyboy tactics and slapping us in the face. I tell you, that man has been surely seduced by power and has become a Judas."

"Go on."

"The Strike Committee believes he's prejudged the purpose of the strike and has conspired with the Citizens' to end the dispute without a fair settlement."

Sensing a scoop, Patterson arched a surprised eyebrow. "Do you have any proof of this?"

"Not yet."

"Perhaps then you're the ones prejudging. Didn't Robertson successfully intervene in the general strike here last year and talk city officials into a settlement acceptable to workers?"

"Yes, he did," conceded Russell.

Patterson flipped his notepad to a fresh page. "Can you assure me, my paper and the people back East you've no intention of Soviet rule here and aren't in contact with Bolshevist elements?"

"Well, I support strong means to justify the end, Mr. Patterson, and I won't apologize for that because I'm no friend of the capitalists and their rotten political system. However, I'm a legal member of the Socialist Party of Canada, not a Bolshevik, and I swear there's no red money behind the strike."

"Why a general sympathetic strike? Why not just a walkout by the metal and building trades workers?"

"Wait a second," Russell corrected. "You're missing the point. We're all big boys here and know how to play by rules, but the power-hungry bosses don't. For years they've used everything from scabs to strikebreakers, stool pigeons, court injunctions against picketing and lawsuits to intimidate workers and break legal strikes. It's no wonder Winnipeg is called Injunction City by every workingman with a union card. Employers have relentlessly bullied and threatened workers in this city, so you tell me, Mr. Patterson, how would you deal with this kind of abuse?"

"May I quote you on this?"

Russell bristled. "Certainly, go ahead and print it. What the capitalists don't understand is that workers don't just want a bigger piece of the pie, they want an entirely different pie."

When Patterson looked up from his notes, Russell locked eyes with him. "One more thing. We've had our arses kicked long enough, and we're having none of that stuff anymore. The shoe is now on the other foot, and the truth is the strike is a terrible thing, but there's no turning back because at this point we don't care much for shortcuts. We've been screwed once too often."

He stood, nodding once to Ivens before turning back to Patterson. "Now, I've got to go. There's a lot happening today. Nice meeting you. Thanks in advance for your help."

Chapter 31
Winnipeg
The Strike — Day 15

The president of the Great War Veterans' Association meeting was a hard-driving type with an excellent reputation among Winnipeg's returned men. A former sergeant in the Canadian Expeditionary Force, he was now head of the GWVA's Manitoba Command. Following a series of incidents involving unemployed returned men and foreigners in January 1919, he had been appointed the ex-servicemen's representative on the province's Alien Investigation Board.

Despite these impressive credentials, he was nervous stepping onto the stage in the smoke-filled, stifling-hot hall. A heat wave had been scorching the city for several days, turning Winnipeg into a pressure cooker. That the room was jammed to capacity with veterans, many still in uniform, didn't help.

While the local GWVA executive had endorsed a policy of neutrality on the first day of the strike, the chairman knew the majority of the 10,000-plus members supported the walkout and were increasingly hostile to those who stood in the way of a settlement. Hopefully violence wouldn't be used by the pro-strike men to end the dispute, but he had his doubts that the situation could remain peaceful for much longer.

After waiting a few minutes for the rowdy crowd to come to order, he cleared his throat loudly. "Okay, settle down, men, settle down. Please stand and join our vice-president in the singing of 'God Save the King'."

Hundreds of men were quickly on their feet, lustily singing the familiar anthem to the reigning monarch, George V. Once finished, they sat, and an expectant hush fell as they waited for the meeting to begin.

Near the front of the stage sat a large group of anti-strike returned men who called themselves Loyalists, wearing small Union Jack pins on their jackets. The Loyalists talked a lot about upholding "law and order," but the chairman suspected they had only come to the meeting to find out which veterans supported the red strike leaders.

As the meeting began, it immediately became clear the men wanted something done about the lack of government action to end the strike. Towards the end of a lengthy statement by one veteran, an older man approached the podium and asked to address the men. After verifying his identity, the chairman granted him permission to speak.

Pale-faced and frail-looking, Roger Bray had a receding chin and droopy dark moustache. Since the war ended, he had become a firebrand socialist. "Men," he announced, "I know the strike leaders. They're giving clean, strong, white management of the walkout and are anxious for order. They claim if collective bargaining is granted, the strike will be over in twenty-four hours."

Loud clapping mixed with some booing temporarily interrupted Bray, but he continued. "I say we force the authorities to act, and tomorrow afternoon visit Premier Norris and Mayor Gray in an orderly and lawful manner. We will show them the returned men of Winnipeg demand an end to this strike."

More cheering erupted, drowning out hisses and shouts of "Sit down you goddamn moron!" from the Loyalists.

With one hand on his hip and the other raised over his head, Bray stabbed the air with his forefinger and exclaimed, "We soldiers in the trenches prayed to God Almighty to give us victory, and we pray now. It may be we'll have to use weapons in the fight against capitalism. I say we demand our government leaders persuade stubborn employers and the Citizens' to negotiate with workers in a democratic way."

As Bray paused for breath, one of the Loyalists lurched from his seat, shaking his fist. "Shut up and sit down, Bray, you rotten Bolshevik bastard! You were never in the firing lines and are a disgrace to the uniform."

The outburst silenced the room. Then several Loyalists began to shout.

"Get off the stage, Bray!"

"Let an actual veteran talk for us."

Bray looked down, rolling his eyes. He met the gaze of the first Loyalist, who was still on his feet, right fist raised. "If you don't mind, I have the—" he began.

He never got the last word out. The Loyalist vaulted onto the stage, and in seconds had his hands around Bray's throat. The chairman and vice-president rushed to pry him off. Several other returned men then escorted him from the room while he continued to shout threats.

"Order! Order!" yelled the chairman. It was no use; the room was in uproar. He turned to the vice-president. "Who the hell was that big gorilla who rushed the stage?"

"That's Pat Flanagan, ex-sergeant from the 27th. Everybody calls him Bear. During the fighting, his men couldn't figure out whether he had brass balls or was just plain crazy."

"Why?"

"Once he fell on a grenade thrown by the Germans into the trench where his squad was having a smoke break. Lucky for him, it was a dud. Another time he drew fire from an enemy sniper so one of his own sharpshooters could finish the Hun bastard off."

"Hard to believe."

"It's the God's truth, I swear. He carried a lot of weight with the fellows overseas and still does. Don't you remember last January when the boys raided the Socialist Party office and burned their piano on Smith Street?"

"Sure."

"Bear was in charge. He can be a vicious son of a bitch."

"Wait a minute. Isn't he the same guy who lost his wife and son to the Spanish flu? I heard about him throwing a fit when the hospital tried to have him quarantined."

"Yeah. I wouldn't want to cross him. Bray's lucky he wasn't strangled to death."

Once order was restored, the chairman moved to end the meeting. Before his closing words, he reminded the assembly a *peaceful* visit to Premier Norris and Mayor Gray was scheduled for the next day.

Chapter 32
Winnipeg
The Strike — Day 16

It was night and he was trapped in a mobbed street full of men in army uniforms, broad shoulders jostling. He turned away, but they spotted him. "There he is! There's the coward!" voices shouted. He tried to run, but his legs felt like lead. Suddenly a man with a club was on him. Escape or be killed. He stumbled. The man raised the club. He put up his arm to fend off the blow and screamed —

Patterson jolted upright in a cold sweat, threw off the bed covers and stumbled into the bathroom. In the mirror stared back an unshaven and shaken-looking man. He sank to his knees, gripped the toilet and dry-heaved into the bowl.

Venturing onto the balcony in his bare feet, he was greeted by sticky heat, despite the grey, overcast sky, gusting wind and scudding rain clouds rolling in ominously from the west. As he watched several flags tugging from their poles on downtown buildings, he looked towards the Manitoba Legislature, though it was blocks away. The muggy weather would not be kind to the marchers today.

After learning about the veterans' planned marches to the Legislature and City Hall, Patterson had decided to join them. Despite misgivings about his personal safety, he couldn't afford to be scooped today. *You must be tenacious and dedicated, worth two reporters from any other paper.*

After shaving, dressing and combing his hair, Patterson left the room and walked down to the lobby. Although elevator service was still nonexistent, the hotel had reopened the Selkirk Room. He stood in front of the carved oak desk at the entrance and waited to be seated. In front stretched the elegant restaurant, where hotel patrons and guests couldn't help but be impressed by eight sets of double French doors, woodwork with gold-leaf trimming, and a high, curving-beamed ceiling with skylights and several cut-glass chandeliers. The head waiter courteously seated him in a corner table with a white linen tablecloth and crystal glassware. From this location he could view the courtyard and the entire length of the room.

After ordering breakfast, he read the latest edition of the *Labour News*. The lead story was *Toronto Advocate Backs Strikers*. In it Ivens quoted an editorial by Anderson. *It is becoming more and more clear that the Winnipeg strike is not Bolshevism or any attempt to usurp the government of Canada, but a dispute between employer and employed on the question of wages, hours, union recognition and collective bargaining.*

Following breakfast Patterson took the familiar route on Main to City Hall and Market Square. He pushed the uncomfortable remnants of his dream to the back of his mind and questioned one of the marchers as to how many men were assembled.

"Close to 10,000, I'd guess."

"Who's in charge?"

"The GWVA president is leading the men and Roger Bray is second-in-command."

A light drizzle started as the long procession of ex-soldiers marched with military precision south down Main and west at Broadway Avenue. Patterson slipped into the front ranks. As the men marched past the Fort Garry Hotel and along the wide, tree-lined boulevard, they sang lustily. "We'll Never Let the Old Flag Fail," "Keep the Home Fires Burning" and "Tipperary" were among the clear favourites.

The parade slowed temporarily when it reached Kennedy Street and turned south to the Legislature. Those in the first rows veered off at the yet-unpaved entrance to the building sheathed in Manitoba Tyndall limestone, and marched up its semicircular approach. Halting at the Legislature's front steps, the GWVA president and Bray conferred for a few moments, then signalled the front ranks to enter the building. Behind them a mass of ex-servicemen waited in the rain.

Patterson accompanied the lead group as they climbed the brown-veined Carrara marble Grand Staircase. His eyes were drawn to the two sentinel-like life-size bronze bison at the foot of the stairs and the cut stone panels beneath the second-floor railings resembling the Union Jack.

In the domed antechamber, towered over by four pairs of Corinthian columns, the men temporarily halted. For a moment, they milled on the Tennessee marble floor, before the energy grew too much. Bursting into the empty main chamber, they poured like a waterfall down into the horseshoe arrangement of absentee members' benches. When every desk and chair was taken, the men occupied the Speaker's seat and dais. The next wave were forced to sit on the floor or stand. Soon the doorway was blocked and the Press Gallery filled to capacity.

Searching for a spot in the crowded chamber, Patterson noticed *Free Press*, *Tribune* and *Telegram* reporters in the Press Gallery. Many of the pro-strike soldiers resented the local dailies for their news stories and unfriendly editorials against the workers and the walkout.

Instead of joining his fellow newspapermen, Patterson crouched against the wall near the Speaker's chair. It would be wise to be less visible taking notes.

All around him bedlam prevailed — until Premier Norris suddenly appeared from the crowd and sat at the table below the dais. An expectant, humming silence fell.

Chapter 33
Winnipeg
The Strike — Day 16

"I want you boys in the galleries to behave while I'm speaking and the Premier is replying." The GWVA president went on to remind Norris the returned men in the room had offered their lives for their country and were ready to protect the State and constituted authority.

"I suppose no one in your government has the guts to say we are Bolsehviki," he declared. "The Citizens' Committee has been talking about English and Scotch anarchists, and they've got to be stopped, and you can do it, Mr. Premier. All we want is living conditions and fair wages for our hard work. You may not know this, but some of our comrades are working seventy-four hours a week for fifty and fifty-five dollars a month."

"Shame!"

"Disgrace!"

"Resign!"

"We want collective bargaining as they have it on the railways. Both you and the men here are aware I've had experience in labour negotiations and know there can be no objection to collective bargaining in metal-trade contract shops. That's all we want. The strike can be settled at once on that basis. It has gone on long enough, Mr. Premier, and it's up to the government to take a hand to bring the parties together and force a settlement."

"The government realizes the importance of the question," Norris replied, "and we need no assurance you veterans were not untrue to the State. Although the Legislature isn't sitting right now, the cabinet is this very minute in the middle of an emergency meeting about the strike."

"The time for talking is over!" interjected Bray.

"I understand your frustration and assure you we're doing absolutely everything we can to bring about a fair settlement, but there's a difference of opinion as to what is collective bargaining. Offhand I cannot venture a definition, but you can be certain I'm in sympathy with labour."

"What about the postal employees?" a vet yelled.

"That's a federal matter," replied Norris.

"How about the firemen?" another asked.

"That's up to City Council."

"What about the telephones? They're under your jurisdiction," clamoured a third vet.

"There's no ultimatum in this connection," Norris announced. "Men, though I must return to the cabinet meeting, I promise you prompt and generous consideration." With that he thanked the men for making their views known and began to leave the chamber.

The GWVA president and Bray consulted to decide whether the Premier's answer was satisfactory. Finally, Bray asked for a volunteer to thank Norris for his statement. A young man raised his arm and came forward. "Thank you, Mr. Premier, for your words. However, I want you to understand that time is pressing and we'll be back here tomorrow morning for your answer."

Norris acknowledged the man and exited.

Sitting behind two returned men, Patterson heard one comment, "Is it my imagination or did Norris just give us all the right royal brush-off?"

"You are right. He's stalling," replied his friend. "He's nothing but a two-faced politician buying time. Makes me sick to my stomach that we fought for democracy and now have to put up with this cr—"

"Look in the Press Gallery!" his friend interrupted. "Isn't that the low-life reporter from the Yellowgram who tried to sneak into one of our GWVA meetings and got tossed?"

"Which one?"

"The one with the Union Jack on his coat."

"You're right. What's he doing here?"

"Probably getting ready to print more lies. He's got some nerve coming to our meeting today sporting a Jack."

Patterson looked up towards the Press Gallery and spotted the *Telegram* reporter. Other veterans had also identified the flag-wearing newspaperman and were shouting.

"Take it off! Take it from him!"

Suddenly a nearby returned man jumped from his seat, five feet down into the Press Gallery, and quickly ripped the miniature flag off the reporter's coat. Amidst loud cheers and applause from the nearby men, he glared at the stunned reporter and shouted, "You don't deserve to be here. Get the hell out!"

"I have a — right to be — here," stammered the reporter.

"Not as long as you work for that filthy rag, you don't," exclaimed the veteran.

Patterson's stomach churned. The confrontation would add a dramatic touch for his dispatch on the Legislature's invasion — but it also proved that his reporter's press credentials would not always protect him.

Outside the Legislature thousands of ex-servicemen were waiting on the lawns in the steamy rain for their comrades to return. When Bray emerged he shouted, "Listen up, men, and look lively! We're going to City Hall to visit Mayor Gray."

The men quickly assembled and formed lines behind several large Union Jacks, then on Bray's command about-turned and marched off in columns towards Broadway. Someone started singing "Mademoiselle from Armentières." By the time the men reached Kennedy, their voices could be heard in unison singing the popular wartime song.

Chapter 34
Winnipeg
The Strike — Day 16

Inside City Hall, Mayor Gray was chairing a council session. The motion on the table proposed that no union should exist among the firemen and policemen in affiliation with any other organization.

"The city can do without its striking employees and they should all be fired," declared an anti-strike alderman.

"That won't solve anything," replied Alderman Abraham Heaps.

"We're past 'solving' this. It's time to show —"

The doors burst open. Roger Bray strode in, followed by a delegation of veterans.

"What —"

"Order! Order! We must have order!" Gray's calls were ignored as more veterans squeezed into the room.

A secretary rushed up to him. "Sir, the men outside, the veterans — there's thousands."

Heaps turned to Gray, his face serious. "You're going to have to speak with them, Your Worship. I don't think they'll leave otherwise."

• • •

Emerging onto the front steps, Gray was greeted by a loud chorus of boos and hisses, along with a smattering of handclapping from a crowd of several thousand. He steeled himself.

"The men are waiting, Your Worship," urged Bray.

Gray quickly collected his thoughts. "The returned soldiers did magnificently at the front, and you've done magnificently during the strike."

"Stop the sell-out!"

"End the strike! Force the Citizens' to accept collective bargaining."

"You men know that I can't do that. Before bargaining can begin the strike must be called off and pledges made by all civic employees to never strike again."

Gray's statement was met with more heckles. A chant began. "Resign! Resign!"

"We soldiers in the trenches prayed to God Almighty to give us victory and we pray now," interjected Bray. "Because we know the Citizens' is prolonging the strike, it may be we'll have to take up arms once more for justice. These Citizens' men are out to destroy organized labour, and now the fight is on to the finish."

Loud cheers and yells of *you tell him, Roger* filled the air. Gray stepped forward onto the edge of the parapet. "Men, I'm doing my very best to try and clear up this most difficult situation without violence on our streets. We're attempting to reach some solution which will reestablish normal conditions and at the same time preserve our British institutions of responsible government. However, I appeal to you returned men to exercise patience and calmness. Because the future destiny of Winnipeg may depend upon your wisdom in this grave crisis, I beg you to support constituted authority with your trust, your confidence and if necessary, your all."

With that he retreated.

• • •

By the time Patterson elbowed his way to the front steps, Gray had finished speaking and left amidst a cacophony of jeers and calls for his resignation.

Patterson turned to the nearest man in uniform. "I'm with the *Toronto Advocate*. What do you think of Mayor Gray's comments?"

"Get lost. I'm not interested in talking to the press," the leathery-faced veteran replied.

"How about you?" he asked the man next to him.

"Not a chance."

Patterson spotted Bray, who'd come down from the steps to join the crowd.

"Mr. Bray. William Patterson of the *Toronto Advocate*. Can I please have your reaction to Mayor Gray's comments?"

"Certainly. Is this the thank you returned men are given for their service and sacrifice? We have thousands of men here who carried a pack for our country, and on their return home they believed they were entitled to living conditions and collective bargaining. Prime Minister Borden has suggested the provinces could enact compulsory collective bargaining, and the veterans want prompt action. Also, because officers have remained loyal to duty, most returned men don't support the civic ultimatum that police sign a pledge not to go on sympathetic strike. To force them out now would be trouble."

"What kind of trouble?"

"The kind soldiers can handle."

Patterson jotted down Bray's remarks and moved through the small park to the back of the gathering. Taking shelter from the rain beneath a large statue commemorating the Royal Winnipeg Rifles and the Winnipeggers who died in the 1885 Riel Rebellion, he noticed a man standing across the street waving at him. Curious, Patterson crossed over.

The man was clean-shaven and well dressed, wearing a fedora and fresh wing-tip-collar shirt. "I understand you are a reporter with the *Toronto Advocate*. Is that true?" he asked politely.

"Yes. William Patterson is my name. Who are you?"

"Fred Dixon."

"I have heard a lot about you. Do you want to talk?"

"Yes."

"Swell," said Patterson and took out his notepad.

Dixon shook his head. "Not here. Let's go somewhere where we can converse privately." Dixon led the way down Main until they reached a virtually empty café, where he led Patterson to a back booth.

"Do you mind if I take notes?"

"Not at all."

"Do you think the veterans' parade will make a difference with Norris or Gray?"

"Not much. The provincial government isn't in session and Norris has no intention of recalling it to get involved in the strike. He'll avoid any direct action and defer to the federal and municipal authorities. As for Gray, he'll support the majority on City Council, who oppose the strike."

"What is it that you wish to tell *Advocate* readers?"

"The rejection of increased wages and collective bargaining by Winnipeg employers and the Citizens' is based on long-established exploitation of workers. Most employers fear their profits and control will suffer if their power is lessened. They feel it's fine for the workers to be free, as long as they remain on their knees."

"Go on, please," encouraged Patterson as he scribbled down Dixon's comments.

"For more than twenty-five years the wealthy in Winnipeg have built their dreams on the backs of unskilled workers and poor immigrants, and while they claim their prosperity has been built on self-reliance and ambition, the truth is their success is the result of selfishness, greed and exploitation.

This strike has been a long time coming and is undeniably a just action."

"What about the allegations of Soviet control by radical labour leaders?"

Dixon arched his eyebrows and laughed. "There have been negotiations constantly between the Strike Committee and the city authorities. Does that look like usurpation or Soviet rule? The strikers have gone pretty far and they have made mistakes, but they have not perpetrated Bolshevism. However, by saying 'Bolshevik, Bolshevik, Bolshevik' over and over again, the myth of Bolshevism has been created. As a journalist you know how a particular narrative on a story, repeated over and over again, can eventually become a reality."

"How do you think the strike will end?

"Our political masters have predetermined the strike is a threat to the State. It's only a matter of time before the full weight of government is brought to bear on those labelled revolutionaries. And you know what happens to them?"

"They're eliminated."

"Perhaps, but justice cannot be achieved at the end of a rope."

Dixon stood abruptly and offered his hand to Patterson to shake. Moments later he was gone.

As Patterson headed for the Criterion for a drink, a flat-capped man approached him. "You're Patterson the reporter, aren't you?"

"Yes. Who are you?"

"Never mind that. You need to be careful."

"Careful?"

"You're being watched."

"How do you know this?"

"I'm Ketchen's snitch on the Strike Committee."

Chapter 35
Winnipeg
The Strike — Day 18

Patterson waited in the lobby of the Oxford Hotel for Abraham Heaps. Peering out the window, he watched a young couple strolling arm and arm towards Market Square pass Heaps, who was coming up the street.

Before he could reach the Oxford, Heaps was stopped by several workers in dark coveralls and cotton work shirts. Friendly greetings and handshakes were exchanged, followed by several minutes of conversation. Heaps did most of the talking, occasionally patting the palm of one hand with the back of the other to make a point. One of the men said something, evidently funny, provoking considerable laughter. Heaps pointed to his watch, left the men and entered the Oxford.

"Good morning, Mr. Heaps," greeted Patterson. "Given how busy you are, I appreciate you taking time for an interview."

"Please call me Abe," Heaps replied with an easy smile as he shook Patterson's hand. "I asked to meet here so you could see the Labour Café and meet its driving force — the young women's protectress, Helen Armstrong. She'll be here in a little while, but until then I'll be happy to answer questions."

"Do you mind going on the record?"

"Not at all."

Before Patterson could take out his notepad, a petite and attractive woman in her early twenties wearing a plain working shift and a white apron approached the table. She had a slim figure, a cute turned-up nose sprinkled with freckles, rosy lips and sparkling green eyes. However, her most striking feature, suggesting Irish descent, was red hair spilling out over her shoulders in long curls.

"Good morning, Alderman Heaps," she said pleasantly, lips parted in a warm smile. "What brings you and your friend here?"

"Well, I'll do just about anything for a cup of coffee served by one of Winnipeg's prettiest ladies and, I might add, queen of the two-step dance."

"Enough of your flattery. You're making me blush," she bantered. "And coming from a married man, you should be ashamed of yourself."

They laughed. "I am indeed," Heaps replied, eyeing the young woman affectionately. "Amy, I would like you to meet Mr. William Patterson. Mr. Patterson, meet Amy Wells."

"Good morning," Patterson said smiling.

"Good morning, Mr. Patterson." Wells beamed, revealing a dimple on her right cheek.

"Please call me Will. I'm a reporter with the *Toronto Advocate*, sent to cover the strike."

"Well, that explains why you're here with Alderman Heaps. Now, what can I get you gentlemen?"

"Two coffees, please," Heaps replied.

After Wells left, Patterson began to ask his first question, but Heaps put up his hand. "Amy may be a looker, Mr. Patterson, but she's also a hard worker. She hasn't missed a day at the Café since it opened."

"Thank you," Patterson remarked. "Now, can we begin?"

Ignoring the question, Heaps continued, "Before the strike, do you know how much Amy made a month as a waitress at the Kensington Café?"

"No."

"Fifteen dollars a month."

"You're kidding me."

"Actually it was nine dollars."

"How could it be that low?"

"She worked from seven o'clock in the morning until two in the afternoon and then returned for the rest of her shift between five and midnight — a total of thirteen hours per day, for which she was paid fifteen dollars a month, with three days off. However, she had to pay one dollar per week for laundry and fifty cents per week to the busboy, so in the end each month she had nine dollars to pay room rent, clothes, recreation and outdoor meals."

"She's one pay envelope from starvation, isn't she?"

"Yes," Heaps agreed. "Then there's Sid. He worked from eight o'clock at night to seven the next morning, six days a week, in an office building, cleaning seven floors, five lavatories and all the glass and brass work. He ran the elevator from seven until nine in the morning and on Saturday tended to the furnace. His wages were fifty dollars a month."

"He's exploited too."

"Right. Now, let me answer your questions."

"What brought you into politics?"

"I felt I could make a difference to thousands north of the tracks. When I looked around my neighbourhood I saw plenty of brothels, noisy bars, flophouses and filthy factories but not enough schools, clinics and parks. After Fred Dixon was elected to the Legislature, I spoke with him about my own chances. He convinced me to run in Ward Five at the next opportunity, and the rest, Mr. Patterson, is history. Together with Alderman Queen, we represent over 80 percent of the Jewish, Ukrainian and Polish voters in the city, more than 60 percent of the Germans and Scandinavians and about 15 percent of the Anglo-Saxons."

"Care to comment on statements by the Citizens' that your North End ward is full of Bolshevik sympathizers behind the strike?"

"This is part of the organization's smear tactics. While it's fair to say many from this section of the city support the strike, there are few if any Bolsheviks. Quite honestly, Mr. Patterson, most immigrants are hard workers who have been ruthlessly exploited in the past and now are being used as scapegoats."

"I suppose you've heard the rumour that immigrants have spread the Spanish flu in Winnipeg."

"Yes I have," he replied, his voice sharpening. "It's ridiculous. What *is* true is that working-class neighbourhoods have faced the greatest devastation from the epidemic and immigrants have suffered the most."

"Why?"

"Having wealth means better living conditions and sanitation, which limits spread of the disease. It also means those who did become ill had greater access to health care. Immigrant families have neither proper living conditions nor sanitation."

Amy Wells returned with the coffees. Patterson looked up. She smiled. Was the smile for him?

"The strike's almost three weeks old," said Patterson. "Are you surprised it has lasted this long?"

"No."

"Will it succeed?"

"Depends what you mean by *succeed*. It has already proven workers have more power when they're united."

"So is the strike about wages, working conditions and union recognition, or about wresting control from the bosses?"

"Both. Power is in the hands of the Anglo-Saxon business leaders in Winnipeg, and all the heated debates in the last year within City Council have derived from this reality."

"Senator Robertson has returned to Ottawa, but before leaving he was quoted as saying, 'The promoters of the general strike in Winnipeg now sit in the ashes of their folly.' What's your reaction to his statement?"

"What ashes? What folly? There continues to be remarkable solidarity among the strikers, who, together with their families, represent more than half of the city's population."

"A final question. How will workers feel if the strike fails?"

"They'll lose all hope for justice and be bitter for decades."

As Patterson closed his notepad and thanked Heaps, Helen Armstrong entered the Labour Café.

Chapter 36
Winnipeg
The Strike — Day 18

Helen Armstrong was a tempest of a woman. She had a wide mouth set in a rather plain face, a strong chin and dark, mischievous eyes that revealed an intense nature and quick intelligence. Known to the women at the Labour Café as Ma, Armstrong was tough, big-hearted and sharp-tongued. She was also famously unafraid of authority and believed apologizing to employers was a sign of weakness.

"I would like you to meet Mr. William Patterson, a reporter with the *Toronto Advocate*," said Heaps.

"We've already met," Armstrong replied. "At City Hall before the strike started."

"Good morning, Mrs. Armstrong. Nice to see you again."

She placed her hands on her hips. "You wish to ask some questions."

Not one to waste time. "Yes."

"Go ahead, but be brief. We're about to prepare lunch."

Patterson removed his notepad, noting by her reaction she had no objection. "Please tell our readers a little about yourself."

"I was born in Toronto and raised in a working-class family. My father was a member of the Knights of Labour, and when I was young I worked in his tailoring shop. I met George, who was a carpenter, and we were married in Toronto. First we moved to the United States, and then came to Winnipeg. By the time we established ourselves here, we had four children."

"Can you summarize your involvement in labour organizing and politics in Winnipeg?"

"It started in early 1917 when I helped revive Winnipeg's Women's Labour League and organized the Retail Clerks' Union. Soon after, I led Woolworth's women clerks out on strike. The next year I organized the Hotel and Household Workers' Union, and this year the city's biscuit-factory workers, laundry workers and knitting-machine operators."

"How did you do all of this and raise four children?"

She seemed amused. "George and I share raising the children, and when we both need to be away, the older girls look after their brother."

"George is also involved in the strike."

"He's on the Strike Committee."

"So are you, right?"

"Yes. I represent the Women's Labour League."

"You've been described by some as a radical activist and feminist. How do you respond to this claim?"

"I have a strong belief in the equality of men and women, and I'm adamant about empowering women to fight for themselves. Frankly, Mr. Patterson, women, like men, have to learn to fight, as men in the master class have done, to protect their interests. The lives of many of our working girls are so unbearable that in the end the street claims them as easy prey. The most recent attempt by a local employer at manipulation has been bribery."

"Bribery?"

"The day the strike began, Eaton's gave its largely female staff an unexpected and large salary increase, but despite this 'incentive,' 900 of the company's women employees joined the strike."

"How many women strikers are there?"

"Thousands."

"*Thousands?*"

"Yes. For example, the day after the strike started, over 1,000 women service workers alone joined the strike, and a few days later 500 women employed at Eaton's formed picket lines in front of the store."

Patterson scribbled down the information, then asked a question he knew would be of interest to the paper's readers. "Since the strike began, you've been arrested for disorderly conduct, unlawful assembly and inciting strikers."

"Yes."

"Under what circumstances?"

"Intimidating scabs at factory gates, in front of retail stores and on street corners selling newspapers, and encouraging women to block delivery wagons into their neighbourhoods without Strike Committee permission signs."

"The *Citizen* paper has labelled you *the female Bolsheviki*."

"I don't care what that paper thinks of me."

"Were you scared when the police arrested you the first time?"

"No."

"Why not?"

"I was walking a picket line, which, as you know, is a legitimate activity."

"What about when you were arraigned in court?"

"I'm not the least bit afraid to face a magistrate and defend this right. Furthermore, if going to jail is necessary to combat oppression, then I'm willing to do so. However, I'm not willing to be bullied. Never have been."

"Let's finish with the Labour Café. Why did you establish it?"

"I realized women who left their jobs to join the strike needed a place to receive food and help with money to pay rent. At first the Café was located in the Strathcona Hotel at

Rupert and Main. Good-natured owner Mr. Rosenthal made available the kitchens and dining rooms. However, under pressure from the Citizens', after ten days it was forced to go elsewhere. I turned to the strikers' Relief Committee and the Labour Church for funds to relocate the Café in bigger and better downtown quarters. Fortunately the Oxford's owner offered his hotel to us."

"Can you describe the food kitchen?"

"It's staffed by 200 volunteers and offers three meals a day. We're now serving 1,500 people daily, mostly striking women from department stores, laundries, garment factories, restaurants and candy kitchens. We also offer cash grants for the same workers to meet room rent and provide meals to women and children of the men strikers."

A Café volunteer approached Armstrong and whispered something to her.

"I must go now, Mr. Patterson. Something has come up that needs my attention."

"I understand. Thank you for the interview."

"You're welcome."

Heaps rejoined Patterson. "What do you make of Helen?" he asked.

"One tough woman," Patterson replied. "I get the impression if someone barked at her, she would simply bark back."

Heaps chuckled. "Helen's more than tough. She's indestructible."

Leaving the Café, Patterson noticed a group of young people gathered at a bulletin board, reading a notice.

To girls and boys. Line up here tomorrow for picket duty at 7:30. Protect your job. Employers' notices are all bluff.
Mrs. Helen Armstrong

Chapter 37
Winnipeg
The Strike — Day 21

Helen Armstrong entered the Labour Temple and walked down the first-floor hallway to her office. It was spartan — a steel desk, two wooden chairs and a three-level filing cabinet. On the walls were framed pictures of several former WTLC presidents and a large cork bulletin board displaying a city map and announcements from the various strike committees.

Easing into her chair, she began to read the new announcements. The Strike Committee had again closed restaurants and movie houses and discontinued bread and milk delivery. While she expected a tremendous run on the stores for supplies and bitter criticism in the *Citizen* and the local papers, she hadn't anticipated two other results. Municipal officials had taken over responsibility for milk delivery, making this essential available at most Winnipeg schools, and while the regular police force was still on the job, the city had secured 500 "special" constables to protect food workers and bakery and creamery plants.

On her desk was a message from Ivens warning that the constant marches by pro- and anti-strike returned men were raising the stakes for the Strike Committee, veterans, the Citizens' Committee and the authorities. He predicted Gray was going to issue an order banning all parades and forbidding congregation of crowds on city streets. If marches were going to be banned, Ivens wanted a location where the ex-servicemen, workers and their supporters could legally assemble. Armstrong grimaced. Not finding an alternative for large-scale gatherings might be a major blow to the strike because they were crucial to providing information, maintaining morale and raising funds.

She stared at the map on the bulletin board. The ideal place was Victoria Park. The tree-lined open space south of Pacific Avenue along the Red River was big enough to accommodate large crowds, and its stage could be used for speakers. Equally important, the park was only a few blocks from the Labour Temple, City Hall, Main Street and Market Square. After scribbling a reply to Ivens about the location, Armstrong left again for the Labour Café to prepare lunch for the growing number of strikers and their families.

Chapter 38
Winnipeg
The Strike — Day 21

The parade of several hundred Loyalists slowly approached Market Square. Bear strode in front, where a half dozen men carried a large banner proclaiming *We Will Maintain Constituted Authority, Law and Order*. Further back, other anti-strike veterans held signs declaring *Down with Bolshevism, To Hell with the Alien Enemy* and *God Save the King*. When the parade ended at the Square, a large contingent of the marchers gathered on William Street in front of the Leland Hotel.

Then a shout rose from the crowd. "C'mon, some of our fellows are busting up a pro-strike demonstration in front of City Hall!"

• • •

Walking down Main, Armstrong noticed a large number of veterans in the small park fronting City Hall. Their pro-strike banners announced *We Stand 35,000 Against One Thousand, Britons Shall Never Be Slaves* and *We Fought the Hun Over There, and We Will Fight the Hun Everywhere*. Two returned men had climbed up the statue of the Little Black Devils and unfolded a sign reading *Up With Liberty, Down With Oppression*.

By the time Armstrong reached the park, dozens of Union Jack–wearing Loyalists and a police squad were converging on the scene.

Patterson was stationed across Main, in front of Pantages Theatre. Next to him was a photographer. When the camera-wielding man saw the police and Loyalists moving towards the park, he spoke. "There's going to be trouble."

"It was bound to happen," replied Patterson, and stepped off the sidewalk.

"Hey, mister! What the hell are you doing? If you go over there, you're going to get hurt — or arrested."

Ignoring the warning, Patterson crossed Main.

It didn't take him long to spot Armstrong. She was the only woman in the crowd.

As the police tackled a pair of fighters in front of her, two Loyalists closed in. She elbowed the first one, then spread her feet apart and clenched her fists for a fight with the second.

Armstrong stepped forward and spit on him. "Take that, you bastard!"

Helen Armstrong confronts Bear.

Before he could do anything, two officers pinned his arms and pulled him away.

A constable grabbed her. "That's enough, Mrs. Armstrong. You don't want to scuffle with Bear, he's as mad as his nickname."

"Get your hands off of me!" she screamed, and pushed him back.

"That's it! You're under arrest."

"Why?" She glared at the officer, crossing her arms over her chest.

"Disorderly conduct, rioting, intimidation, unlawful assembly and assaulting a policeman."

"I've a right to be here!"

"Not when you're counselling and inciting others to disturb the peace. Now come along and don't give us any more trouble, or you'll also be charged with resisting arrest."

• • •

As they hustled Armstrong away, Patterson caught up to her.

"Are you okay?"

Over her shoulder she shouted, "Yes. Tell George the police have taken me to the Rupert station. He'll know what to do."

Patterson looked for an interview, but no one wanted to talk. Eventually an officer forced him back across the street.

"Who *are* you, mister?" said the photographer, who hadn't moved.

"William Patterson, *Toronto Advocate*."

"Do you know who the arrested woman is?"

"Helen Armstrong," replied Patterson.

"No, sir. She's the Wild Woman of the West."

Chapter 39
Winnipeg
The Strike — Day 22

O ver breakfast at the Venice, Patterson read the local press reaction to the Strike Committee's decision to once again suspend delivery of milk and bread. Under the headline *Declare War on the Babies*, the *Telegram* lashed out. *To resume the former attitude of non-delivery, therefore, is knowingly to conspire to commit child-murder. By the decision to stop the deliveries of milk and bread, the strike leaders have declared war upon babies.*

Under *Baby Killing*, the *Free Press* also attacked the decision. *The renewed interruption of the supply of milk and bread to householders of Winnipeg brings uppermost the question of responsibility for the rise in the rate of infantile mortality which will inevitably accompany it. If the number of deaths among children through deprivation of the accustomed supply of milk increases, these additional deaths will be at the door of the strike committee.*

In contrast, the *Labour News* cautioned, *Strikers, Hold Your Horses! This is the hour when you can win. Steady Boys Steady, Keep Quiet, Do Nothing, Keep Out of Trouble, Don't Carry Weapons, Leave this to your enemies, Continue to prove that you are the friends of law and order.*

After an unsuccessful attempt at obtaining information at City Hall and the Labour Temple, Patterson returned to the Alex. Waiting for him was a message from Davies.

I have some very valuable information to trade. If you're interested, meet me at the Criterion tonight at 8.

Davies

At first he was inclined to ignore Davies's message. *But what if Davies has something big, such as a Citizens' membership list? Or details of a plan to arrest strike leaders? Perhaps proof that red money is behind the walkout?*

Davies was a heavy drinker. Maybe after one too many whiskies he would share his *valuable information* in return for little or nothing. If the information proved valuable, it might make a good story. If it was very valuable, it might result in a scoop. The risky part was not to drink as much as Davies, or arouse his suspicion. *Maybe if I give the guy a head start . . .*

An hour after the appointed meeting time, Patterson arrived at the Criterion.

"Jesus, Patterson, where the hell have you been?" growled Davies, who removed his hairpiece and tossed it on the table.

"Sorry for being late, but something came up at the last minute," lied Patterson. He noted the Colonel's empty glass and flushed face. *So far, so good.*

"I was beginning to think you wouldn't come."

"Your message intrigued me. That's why I'm here."

"Right. Well before we get started, let's have a drink."

"Sure."

Davies caught the bartender's attention. "Two whiskies, Sam."

"Your money's no good tonight. Drinks are on me," said Patterson.

"Well, that's big of you."

"I've a reason for doing it. You want to trade information but I may not have much to offer, so they're on me."

"Mighty generous of you."

When the drinks arrived, Davies clinked Patterson's glass and announced, "Here's mud in your eye," and quickly downed half. Patterson took much less.

"I've been snooping around Minto and Fort Osborne Barracks," Davies began. "Both are scrubbed clean and full of men. I saw General Ketchen there, complete with pressed uniform, sidearm and swagger stick. Christ, all he was missing was a monocle and a batman."

Davies pulled out a thick cigar, licked the end and put it in his mouth. "Ketchen's tighter than a lid on a rusty jar, and some of the lads joke the brigadier sees a halo over his head when he shaves, but for my money he's getting results. He has hundreds of fresh militia. They get housed and fed by the government for several days, receive riot training and then are sent home."

"Sent home? That doesn't make sense. What happens if there's trouble?"

"Ketchen has organized sirens and steam whistles on top of several buildings, including the *Free Press*, Eaton's and Vulcan Ironworks. If the men have to be called out quickly, the sirens and whistles sound the return to barracks and presto, he has a small army."

Davies lit his cigar and took a deep drag, letting the smoke fill his lungs then drift out his nostrils. Soon a dense cloud of bluish smoke hung in the air over his bare head. "Fortunately I spotted an old poker pal, a demobbed senior officer. He shared some very interesting information."

"Is he a reliable source?"

"You bet," confirmed Davies, smiling. "He's the kind of guy who believes an officer's word is a sacred trust, but to be sure, I slipped him a few bucks."

"What did he tell you?"

"Ketchen has been very busy quietly building up forces from the Royal Winnipeg Rifles, Winnipeg Grenadiers, Winnipeg Light Infantry and the Queen's Own Cameron Highlanders. He's also had twenty Lewis light automatic machine guns secretly sent by train from Montreal. Had them put in crates labelled *Regimental Baggage, 27th Battalion* and shipped right under the noses of the CPR's union baggage handlers. Ain't that rich?"

"Anything else?"

"He has an armoured car at Fort Osborne, equipped with three of the Lewis guns, and two mobile militia units, one at each barracks, complete with a troop of Fort Garry Horse and infantry escorts in trucks."

Davies emptied his glass. When Patterson said nothing, Davies tossed his half-finished cigar to the floor, crushed it with his shoe, then spat accurately into the brass spittoon next to the bar rail. "Now, before you give me something, Patterson, I have to piss. Drink up and order two more."

As soon as Davies was out of sight, Patterson grabbed both glasses and went to the bar. He carefully emptied his own nearly full glass into the spittoon and ordered two fresh whiskies.

When Davies returned to the table, Patterson was ready to do something unethical but necessary.

"Now, what can you offer?"

"First, I already know most of what you just told me," Patterson lied with a straight face.

Davies blinked. "What do you mean?"

"I've interviewed Alderman Heaps and he revealed the strikers know all the actions contemplated by the military, their strength, equipment and armament."

"I don't believe you. Did he have proof?"

"Yep. The strikers have had a spy in the GNWT office since the start of the strike. He provides copies of all wires forwarded or received and sends them to the Strike Committee." Patterson took a sip of his whisky. "So now tell me something I don't already know."

"How about this?" Davies replied with a self-satisfied look. "It's about the Citizens' ads in the *Free Press*, *Tribune* and *Telegram*."

Patterson had seen several of the anti-strike ads and had been astounded at their racist and slanderous content. "What about them?"

Davies took a long drink, then lowered his glass. "The newspapers are running them free for now, with payment when the strike's over."

"Who's writing the ads?"

"They won't tell me. I'm not asking, and my advice is to not pursue this any further."

"Aren't you curious to know? I sure would be. It's pretty wild stuff."

Davies balked. "Look, I'm curious about crocodiles too, but I don't want to stick my head in their mouths. Get my point. Sometimes in this town it's best to let certain people do what they want regardless of whether their actions are really right or wrong. Ivens, Russell and their Bolshie friends gagged all three papers soon after the walkout began. I heard Dafoe had to be peeled off the bejesus ceiling when he showed up to find the *Free Press* closed by the strike. By Christ, if they had shut down my freelancing, I'd be mad as hell too."

Davies was red-faced and drooling, but Patterson couldn't tell if he was drunk, because the man seemed to defy normal limits of alcohol consumption. Regardless, it was time to end the meeting. "Look, I agree it's not surprising the local dailies have published the Citizens' ads. No one expects them not to retaliate."

"Maybe, but I have more —"

"No thanks," Patterson cut him off and waved a dismissive hand. "Don't waste your breath. Perhaps the next time you will have some real news."

"You're not leaving, are you?" he slurred.

Patterson broke eye contact and abruptly stood up.

"You ungrateful son of a bitch!" snapped Davies, giving Patterson a withering look as he left the table. "There won't be a next time."

Chapter 40
Winnipeg
The Strike — Day 25

Patterson strolled through Victoria Park. High above, a hawk swooped and soared, catching air currents over the relatively calm waters of the Red River. He had walked to the riverbank from the pumping station, with its large arched windows and corbelled brick bands. Now from the water's edge he could see across St. Boniface and further up, to a bend in the Red where it curved in a wide arc around Point Douglas.

After enjoying several minutes of early-morning peace and quiet near a copse of trees, Patterson retraced his steps to the middle of the park, where a crowd of ex-servicemen and a large number of strikers were gathering in front of an open-air platform. The planked stage was the location for almost daily speeches by pro-strike representatives. As usual the vast majority in the crowd were men, though a few women were scattered here and there. Several uniformed returned soldiers were already moving through the crowd, passing hats to collect money for the Labour Café.

General Ketchen was scheduled to speak first, and Patterson needed to capture his remarks about Mayor Gray's ban on marches and public demonstrations. Another contentious issue Ketchen would likely address was the dismissal of almost the entire police force and hiring of special police. While returned men were upset about the ban on marches, they were even angrier over the armband-clad specials, not only because they were allowed to carry clubs but because they were being paid six dollars per day, twice the temporary discharge allowance given to veterans.

At precisely 9:00 a.m. Ketchen mounted the wooden ladder at the back of the stage. With a full dress and immaculately smart uniform, peaked cap, polished leather boots and swagger stick, a neatly trimmed moustache and tanned face, he radiated the very image of a professional soldier. Striding across the platform, he came to attention on the front edge of the stage, cleared his throat and began to address the crowd.

"As commander of Military District Number 10 Winnipeg, my responsibility is to organize and maintain a militia for the disposal of the federal government at all times. One of those times is now, and so I've come here to request loyal citizens committed to upholding law and order in this city to volunteer for duty."

Patterson heard some cheering, but when it died down a veteran yelled, "What are you going to do about the reds?"

"All undesirables, whether they be reds, Bolsheviks, alien enemies, agitators or disloyal returned men who have chosen the primrose path to revolution and law-breaking, will be severely punished."

"What about the high cost of living?" asked another.

"The high cost of living is intolerable and the government should be using the War Measures Act to deal with this situation."

"Do you support the mayor's ban on parades?" shouted a veteran.

"Yes, and let me explain why. At first the marches were conducted with order and discipline, as befitting former military men of merit and good conduct. There was no pushing, no anger. However, subsequent reckless actions by a handful of demobilized men have caused deep concern to Mayor Gray and the City Council and resulted in many complaints of intimidation and harassment from private citizens, business owners and government officials. Therefore the mayor has imposed a ban on all parades and mass demonstrations on the streets, and while I personally deplore the need for such a drastic measure, I completely support this decision."

"What about the specials? We don't want strikebreakers," urged a flat-capped worker.

Patterson leaned forward. Ketchen's answer was critical.

"The special constables have been recruited because the regular police officers have abandoned their responsibilities to the citizens of this city and refused to sign a pledge required by the Police Commission never to join in sympathy strikes again. The mayor was given no choice but to turn to loyal-minded men to prevent lawlessness and disorder. I am proud to say that among those who have offered their services are scores of patriotic men who recently served our country overseas." With this explanation Ketchen left the stage and walked back to the park's entrance, where his Model T Ford and driver, as well as a special, were waiting.

Patterson hurried around the platform, hoping to catch Ketchen for an interview, and caught up with him just as he was entering his automobile.

"William Patterson, *Toronto Advocate*. May I have a few words, General?"

Ketchen ignored him and ordered his driver to leave.

Patterson turned to the special. "Too bad I missed him. Do you know where I can find him?"

"At Osborne Barracks," replied the special, tapping the end of his club in his free hand.

"I see by the armband and badge you're a special. What's your name?"

"Call me Bear."

Chapter 41
Winnipeg
The Strike — Day 25

"Can I ask a few questions?" said Patterson.

"No," said Bear gruffly, and began walking away. He didn't really want to talk.

Patterson caught up to him. "It won't take long."

Bear hesitated. *Maybe if I give the man something he'll leave me alone.* ". . . I'll give you two minutes. That's it."

"Thank you," said Patterson, removing his notepad. "Why did you become a special?"

"General Ketchen told us the regular police had broken sworn promises to uphold the law and were being controlled by the strikers. Since they were going to be fired, he needed a force of loyal men to prevent disorder. Some of us veterans decided red strike leaders and foreigners shouldn't be in charge anymore, so we joined up."

"What battalion did you serve with?"

"The 27th. What about you? Were you overseas?"

"Sort of," Patterson answered uneasily.

"What do you mean?" Bear bristled. "You were either there or not."

"I was in England working as a foreign service officer for the Canadian government. My job was to help our country's war effort, but I came no closer than London to the action."

"Lucky bastard."

"I guess you could say so."

"I have to go back to the barracks now—"

"One more question. What makes you think reds are behind the strike?"

This guy won't quit. Time to level with him. "Everyone knows while we were fighting and dying in France, Bolsheviks, socialists and enemy aliens infiltrated the country, took our jobs and are now behind the labour troubles. After we returned home and couldn't find work, we decided to do something about it. We roughed them up at Market Square and then wrecked their headquarters. It felt good to take action."

"Why do you hate them so much?"

"You would never understand."

"Try me," Patterson challenged.

Why not, thought Bear. "During the war I learned to hate when my pals got shot. It was hard getting to be like that, feeling I loathed the enemy so badly I was willing to kill them with my bare hands if necessary. But after a while I came to understand it wasn't really hate driving me but fear. Either I killed them or they killed me. Sounds cruel and inhuman, but it's true. Besides, no matter what the politicians, generals and medal winners say, there is precious little glory in the trenches and absolutely no valour in sudden death."

Patterson nodded. "Why did you enlist?"

"Most of my friends went overseas and I didn't want to be left behind and called a coward. Besides, everybody said the war would be over by Christmas."

"Were you prepared for what happened in France and Belgium?"

"Not a chance! War was hell, and those who survived the bullets, bayonets, infections, trench foot and rats will never be the same again. Guys shot themselves to avoid action, and I saw an officer mercy-kill a man with his guts hanging out."

Bear paused. His head felt hot, gut beginning to churn.

"But you're home now. The war's over."

"Yeah, and we thought things would be different. You know, a better life. But now the reds and Bolsheviks are threatening the very things we fought and died for. So I won't hesitate to take up a rifle to defend my family and country from these bastards. Do you get it now?"

"No, tell me."

"Life back here is no different than being in the trenches. Who will survive, us or them?"

They had reached Main. Bear stopped and faced Patterson. "Let me ask you a question."

"Sure."

"Whose side in the strike are you on?"

"I'm on nobody's side."

"How's that possible? You're either for or against it."

"I'm a newspaperman. My job is not to choose sides but to report the facts."

Silence hung between them for several seconds.

Tapping his club in his open hand and raising his eyebrows, Bear stared hard at Patterson. "Let me give you some advice, Patterson. This strike isn't going to end peaceably, and when it does, make sure you're not at the wrong end of one of these, or a bullet."

Chapter 42
Winnipeg
The Strike — Day 26

Bear adjusted the stirrups, grabbed the pommel and smoothly lifted himself up onto the mare's old stock saddle. The four-year-old chestnut provided by Eaton's was unaccustomed to carrying a heavy rider, but Bear had a way with horses and quickly calmed her down.

"Whoa, girl, it's all right. Bear will take good care of you," he whispered while stroking her withers. "Let's get used to each other."

He pulled lightly on the mare's reins and touched her flanks with his knees to lead her into a slow trot, then slipped the reins into his left hand so his right could be free. "That's a girl, now you have it," he said reassuringly.

Adjusting himself in the saddle, Bear recalled how he had joined the mounted troop of specials.

First he had been sworn in. "Please place your hand on the Bible, Mr. Flanagan, and repeat after me," the City clerk had intoned.

"I solemnly swear to uphold the law and faithfully protect and serve the citizens of Winnipeg, so help me God," Bear parroted.

"Thank you. You are now a deputized special constable of the city of Winnipeg. Here's your badge and an armband, which you need to wear while on duty. You will be paid six dollars per day, courtesy of the City." Bear took the white City SP armband and slipped it over the sleeve of his jacket. Then the clerk surprised him. "Can you ride?"

"Pardon me?"

"Can you ride a horse, son?"

"Yes, sir."

"Good. Go see the pipe-smoking gentleman there at the counter."

Bear approached the distinguished-looking man. He had short hair, a pencil-thin moustache, steel-grey eyes and a square jaw, and despite the warm weather he was wearing a Norfolk jacket and a linen shirt. "The clerk told me to see you," announced Bear.

"What's your name, son?" said the man in an authoritative voice. Something in his bearing told Bear the man was ex-military and likely an officer; something in his accent suggested British heritage.

"Pat Flanagan, sir, but my pals call me Bear."

"I can see why. Were you overseas?"

"Yes sir. A sergeant with the 27th."

"Which engagements?"

"Passchendaele, Ypres and a whole lot of other places I would as soon forget."

The man gave Bear a knowing look. "I know what you mean." He paused, then asked, "Now, can you really handle a horse, sergeant?"

"Yes, sir. I grew up on a farm and learned to ride early. Fact is, I'm more at ease on a nag than a bicycle."

"Good, because you're going to be on one again."

Soon afterwards, Bear was assigned to the specials' mounted detail. Today was its first patrol.

A question from the troop's commanding officer interrupted Bear's thoughts. "Comfortable up there?"

"Yes, sir."

"Good. Today we're going to show these damn strikers who owns the streets. Take this, you may need it," he said and handed Bear a long wooden baton.

"It's awful heavy!' Bear exclaimed as he held the long club in his right hand. "What did you do to it?"

The officer smiled. "A little trick I learned working for a blacksmith. You core out a good-sized hole in the top of the yoke and pour in some melted lead. Once it hardens you have a lot more weight when you swing it. I call this my *persuader*. Give the business end of this baby to some red bastard and he won't give you any trouble."

Chapter 43
Winnipeg
The Strike — Day 26

Patterson held up a crumpled copy of Mayor Gray's recent decree and read it again as the elevator descended to the ground floor of the Alex.

> *Proclamation*
> *By virtue of the authority vested in me I do hereby order that all persons do refrain from forming or taking part in any parades or congregating in crowds in or upon any of the streets of the City of Winnipeg, and hereby request of all law abiding citizens the full compliance with this proclamation.*
>
> CHARLES F. GRAY, *Mayor*
> GOD SAVE THE KING

So far the proclamation had been effective in preventing returned soldiers' parades. Coupled with this development, hundreds of special police, many Loyalists, were now patrolling the streets in twos and threes, guarding milk-delivery wagons and making sure workers and pro-strike veterans confined mass gatherings to Victoria Park.

Exiting the elevator, Patterson walked through the lobby, and as he passed the entrance to the Selkirk Room, one of the dining-room stewards greeted him. "Good-day, Mr. Patterson. Will you be having lunch today? I can find you a quiet corner table if you like."

"Not this afternoon, thank you."

At the front desk Patterson enquired if there were any telegrams.

"No, sir. Headed out for a walk?"

"Going downtown."

"Be careful. There may be trouble there today."

If so, there'll also be a story.

Twenty minutes later he arrived to find mass confusion on Main just above Portage. In the absence of streetcars, automobiles and bicycles, hundreds of strikers and their supporters were jamming the sidewalks and spilling out onto the wide thoroughfare. In the middle of the pandemonium, two specials were on traffic duty, struggling to maintain order.

To make matters worse, the two men were being heckled.

"Are you not afraid of being run over?"

"Are you lost?"

Several men in a pool hall above the CV Café were leaning out the windows, letting out wolf-whistles and taunting the two specials.

"Does your mother know where you are?"

"If we wanted clowns, we would have called the Ringling Brothers."

Patterson entered the CV and joined several people gathered at the front window. "What's the commotion?" he asked.

"The traffic specials have been chased away," a man replied. "One of them ran down an alley; the other is hiding in Dingwall's drugstore."

Soon the *clip-clop* of horses was audible above the shouting and blaring of automobile horns.

"Look! More specials!" someone yelled. "A real nasty-looking bunch on horseback with clubs. Christ, they're going to clear the street."

As Patterson watched the approaching riders, three burly men ran into the CV, burst into the kitchen and emerged with empty bottles and containers of eggs. He followed them back out to the sidewalk, where he witnessed them hurl the eggs and glass bottles at the mounted specials.

A roar erupted from the crowd.

Chapter 44
Winnipeg
The Strike — Day 26

Bear was in the first of the two rows of twenty specials. As the troop cantered east on Portage, the mounts' iron horseshoes made a clattering sound as they pounded the streetcar tracks. In front of Bear rode the officer in charge of the detail. Plump, red-faced and sporting a silken moustache, he held one of the heavy clubs in one hand and his horse's reins in the other.

Before the squad left Osborne Barracks, he had given the detail its orders. "We're going on patrol today to test who controls the streets. We'll go east on Portage and north on Main as far as Higgins, then double back to the barracks. You're to remain on your horse at all times and stay in a tight line formation with a short distance between the two rows. Should there be trouble, upon my orders we'll clear the streets and sidewalks, using force if necessary."

• • •

As the troop proceeded on Portage, the number of people on both sides of the street swelled. After they turned north at Main, the specials slowly advanced up the wide street. The riders kept their horses at a slow and steady trot, but soon their snorts and nickers were drowned out by a chorus of shouts and curses from both sides of the street. In the growing chaos the commanding officer ordered the troop to clear everyone off the street. Men, women and children temporarily retreated onto the sidewalks but then quickly closed in on the mounted specials once they passed.

Objects began to fly. Soon riders and horses were hit, and more jeers and hoots filled the air. In the increased frenzy, the specials began to lose control of their mounts as they began to kick and rear under the rain of stones, bricks and bottles. In response the riders used their clubs on anyone within reach.

Ignoring instructions, one special broke ranks and charged into the crowd. No sooner had he reached the sidewalk than a man unseated him from behind. Dropping his club as he fell, the special landed heavily on the ground. Within seconds the crowd was on him.

Seeing him go down, Bear urged his horse forward and, swinging his club in a wide arc, beat a path to where the helpless man lay taking a beating. Dismounting, Bear smashed the nearest attacker in the back. The man fell to the ground screaming and was dragged by friends into a nearby doorway. Bear stood protectively over the moaning special.

"I'm warning you Bolsheviks. I'll cripple the next man who comes close!"

Fists began to fly at him, but Bear held his ground.

• • •

As the fighting morphed into a riot, Patterson stepped out of the CV Café onto the sidewalk. His heart was pounding, but he had to get closer to see anything. He edged down the street, staying as close to the buildings as he could and trying not to get pulled into the heavy crowd.

In a surge by the mounted specials, he saw a woman with a baby carriage get caught. The carriage was crushed, but the mother and baby were rescued. Not as fortunate was another woman slumped on the sidewalk with a glazed and bewildered look. A bystander came limping past him with blood streaming from gashes to his scalp and nose, followed by a rough-looking worker in shapeless, high-waisted trousers, clenching a rider's club.

A few feet away a hulking striker with big, beefy hands scooped up horse manure in his bare hands. "This will teach you scabs to break strikes!" the man screamed and hurled the excrement at a nearby special, catching him squarely in the chest. Another rider was lunging down with his club at a hawk-nosed demonstrator trying to grab the horse's stirrups. The demonstrator yelled, "If you had any guts, you'd get down off that horse and fight like a man, you yellow-bellied scum!"

• • •

Patterson backpedalled away from the fighting. Scanning the street for a safe location, his eyes widened when he spotted Amy Wells, her red hair loose and cascading over her shoulders. She was on the opposite side of the street, shoulders hunched as she took cover behind a newspaper box. Patterson zigzagged through the mass of demonstrators and specials.

"Amy! It's Will Patterson!"

"I remember you," she stammered, her chest heaving and tears streaming down her face.

"This place isn't safe!" he warned.

"Then why are *you* here?"

"I'm a reporter. It's my job. But *you* shouldn't be here."

"My friends are here."

"You'll get hurt. Get out!"

Wells shook her head. "I *have* to stay!"

"Look out!" someone yelled. Patterson turned to see a mounted special bearing down on him. At the last second he jumped aside, narrowly avoiding being trampled. The crowd closed between him and Wells as the rider surged past him to the sidewalk, towards two dismounted riders, one on the ground, the other standing guard over him.

Patterson recognized Bear. The gigantic man was surrounded, lashing out freely with his club. A knife flashed, but Bear sidestepped the thrust and knocked the blade to the ground. Seeing the mounted special coming to Bear's aid, the crowd backed off.

Slowly, the specials began to withdraw and the crowd quieted down. Patterson counted scores of injured strikers, veterans and bystanders. There were broken bones, cuts and lacerations to both sides. *Jesus. The specials completely bungled it.* If that had been crowd control, he would hate to see what an actual offensive looked like.

As he joined a group of stragglers leaving the scene, Patterson came upon Wells with an injured young man.

Special police attack strikers.

"Can I help?"

She replied angrily, "They broke his arm. He needs a doctor."

"Let's take him to the hospital."

"No, they'll ask too many questions. If you *really* want to help, report the truth about what happened today. Make them understand what's at stake now."

She was right. People weren't just afraid of losing their jobs anymore, or even being arrested — they were afraid of being killed.

Chapter 45
Winnipeg
The Strike — Day 27

The Citizens' President, a manufacturer, a lawyer and General Ketchen sat in leather chairs around a mahogany table inlaid with the Board of Trade seal. They were awaiting the arrival of Senator Robertson.

Ketchen was wearing a fresh pressed uniform and sitting ramrod straight in his chair. Despite the high ceiling and several open windows, the room was already uncomfortably warm and filled with smoke from cigars. He fought the urge to cough. *Can we not open a window?*

The President had a nervous habit of juggling several fifty-cent pieces from hand to hand, drawing them out and closing his hands on them. Today, however, he was having trouble with the trick, so he jammed the coins into his pocket and broke the silence. "Let's get on without Robertson."

All agreed. They looked to the President expectantly.

"General, what the hell happened with the mounted specials? From all reports, it was a catastrophe. Foreigners and strikers injured over a dozen of our fine young men. I'm told a Victoria Cross winner is now in a life-threatening condition at Tuxedo!"

Ketchen cleared his throat. "Unfortunately an in-experienced officer was in charge. In all my years in military service, I have never witnessed a more badly planned and deplorably executed operation. The men were simply unprepared for their mission. It was a disaster, especially the manner in which the crowds were controlled."

"Get rid of the officer!" demanded the lawyer, puffing vigorously on his cigar. "But no precipitous withdrawal of the specials. Despite what occurred we need them to patrol the streets, protect property and control strikers."

As the President flicked ashes from his cigar into an elaborate glass ashtray, the discussion turned to the war of words between the *Citizen* and the local dailies against the strikers and their paper.

"The *Citizen* is now providing 25,000 free copies a day and being quoted Dominion-wide in the press," announced the manufacturer. "Our ads in the *Free Press*, *Trib* and *Tely* are showing the strike in its real colour, red. I particularly like *Who Will Get the Jobs, Alien Enemies or War Veterans; Don't Be Misled: The Only Issue Is Bolshevism* and *The Alien Is On His Way Out*."

"Good."

"We need to continue persuading the public the real issue in this dispute is Revolution. Reporters from our local dailies, our good friend Colonel Davies, news hawks from the *New York Times*, *Chicago Tribune* and *Minneapolis Tribune*, and the wire services are supporting our position, informing readers a red element is using the strike to establish a Soviet with Bolshevik principles on the banks of the Red River."

"What else?" said the President, as he took a long pull on his cigar.

"We have convinced American photographer James Hare from *Leslie's Weekly* to take snapshots from the Industrial Bureau for his photo story on the walkout. *Leslie's* is one of the highest-paid circulation magazines in North America, and Hare has indicated his piece will be most sympathetic to our side. He's promised to title the story *Bolshevism in Canada*.

Waiting for the others to absorb his pronouncements, the manufacturer continued, "There's one more item. With the recent bomb attempt on United States Attorney General Alexander Palmer, American press and wire services are very keen to report red activity, a circumstance we must clearly exploit. Frankly, gentlemen, it appears the only press support the strikers have is their propaganda rag, the *Toronto Advocate* and a few small labour publications."

"What about this pesky *Advocate* reporter Patterson?" asked Ketchen. "He's been snooping around for several weeks."

"Why doesn't he go to the Rupert jail and interview that wild Armstrong woman?" joked the President. "I understand she's back in a cell."

"That's rich," offered the lawyer, who had remained largely silent. "Either because she's out on bail or because her henpecked husband already warned him not to."

When the ripple of laughter subsided, the President spoke again. "Patterson writes for a paper few Winnipeg citizens are going to read, and no one from our organization will dare go on the record with him. If he wants information from our side, he can read *our* paper. That way he'll find out exactly what we want."

"Be careful, though. Patterson is not a hack," warned the lawyer.

"So what?" argued the manufacturer. "The strike will collapse any day now, and then he'll be on the first train back to Toronto."

"I hope you're right. However, let's not take any chances," the lawyer insisted.

"What do you mean?"

"We should make him back down."

"What do you suggest?"

"I'll have his room searched, and if evidence of conspiracy with the strike's leaders is found, Patterson will be detained, questioned and arrested."

No one objected to the Citizens' most powerful member.

A short *rap-rap* on the door signalled Robertson's arrival. "Good afternoon, gentlemen. I'm sorry for the lateness."

"We're about to discuss a solution to end the strike," said the President. "Hopefully you've returned from Ottawa with a plan."

"I have. The Borden government believes the strike must end."

"About time," said the President.

Looking at the lawyer for approval, Robertson declared, "Parliament has amended the Immigration Act, permitting deportation without trial for anyone not born or naturalized in Canada who is accused of sedition. With this in mind, I propose a strategy to bring the strike to its knees."

Chapter 46
Winnipeg
The Strike — Day 29

Bear arrived at the Crescent Creamery Company to find the dairy's owner chatting with a group of specials who were ensuring delivery of milk at city schools.

"Here's how you'll proceed," Mr. Carruthers explained. "One of you will drive the rig and the other will ride to prevent trouble."

Bear asked, "Where does the milk come from?"

"It's brought in from the country by farmers in six- and ten-gallon cans and run to our plant from the outskirts by truck. The city allows the dairy to take a profit of one cent on every quart that's sold."

"Is the system working?"

"Pretty much. The first day we tried it, 10,000 quarts were sold. The next day it rose to 15,000."

"What was a normal day before the strike?"

"About 24,000 quarts. Look, I would like to chat longer, but I've got to go. You're doing the right thing by lending us a hand."

Bear joined several specials gathered at the rigs. Some were feeding horses from canvas bags; others stood around smoking or perched on the orange wagons. The rest loaded cases of milk. Many wagons, their shafts in the air, remained idle along the sides of the creamery. One of the specials pointed to a nearby rig. "That one's yours, Bear."

"Thanks," he said and hoisted himself up onto the horse-drawn wagon.

Soon a rugged-looking man dressed in blue overalls and work boots approached the rig. He had a youthful face topped by thick black hair. Climbing up nimbly, he announced, "I'm your driver for today's run."

"Good," responded Bear. "I'm riding shotgun. Name's Pat, but everybody calls me Bear."

"I'm Sean."

"Where are we going today?"

"Aberdeen School in New Jerusalem. Do you know it?"

"No," said Bear. "Never been in the Foreign Quarter before."

"Well, we're headed there today. Corner of Flora Avenue and Salter Street."

"I was told there'll be a special waiting for us at the school."

"That's good —"

"And in case of a disturbance from foreigners," interrupted Bear, "I've something that will prevent anyone tangling with us." He lifted up the tarp at his feet to reveal the heavy club. "I call this my *persuader*."

When Sean didn't react, Bear shrugged.

After a few blocks, Bear broke the silence. "Have you driven one of these rigs before?"

"Before the war I worked a bread wagon."

"Were you overseas?"

"Yep. With the Fort Garry Horse."

"Where did you see action?"

"Moreuil and Rifle Wood and others."

"How long have you been back?"

"Decamped ten days ago."

"You came back in one piece."

"Not really. The doctors at Tuxedo say my hearing will never be the same, and I have shrapnel souvenirs from Fritz in both legs. How about you?"

"Nothing."

"Lucky bastard. Who did you serve with?"

"The 27th."

"See any fighting?"

"Too much."

"No need to say more."

With a tug of the reins, Sean guided the rig along Portage, then turned north at Main. After passing City Hall he continued to Higgins, passed under the subway and entered the North End. At Flora Avenue he turned west.

As they approached the school, Bear noticed a special waiting for them. He gave directions to park the rig in front, where the entrance was barred by tables placed across the doorway. Dropping down, Sean patted the old workhorse, then helped Bear unload the heavy cans of milk. When they were finished, Bear said, "I'm going inside. Stay with the rig."

A few minutes later Bear returned with a large printed sign and placed it on the table in front of the milk.

*Milk Can Be Obtained at This School
Between 10 a.m. and 4:00 p.m. Regular
Prices: Quarts, 13 Cents; Pints, 7 Cents.
Empty Bottles Must Be Brought to
Exchange for Full Ones. By Order.*
Food Committee

"Hope they can read," said Bear.

Chapter 47
Winnipeg
The Strike — Day 29

For two hours Bear and Sean watched children and adults collect their milk supply. Men with small black caps pinned to the backs of their heads spoke softly to kerchiefed women in a guttural language. Two or three children with dark brown skin stood out in the crowd. At one point a young woman and a little girl with a blue blouse and headgear to match asked for bread.

"We don't have any. Now scram!" Bear snapped.

After the woman and child left, Sean asked, "What happens when they don't have a bottle to exchange for milk?"

"Then they're out of luck, though I saw a smart little bugger bring a pail to Gray School yesterday and we filled it with four quarts."

Once the milk supply was exhausted, Bear announced, "We're through here. Time to head back."

On the return trip they ran into trouble twice.

The first time was at Main and Dufferin Avenue, where two foreign-looking men blocked the rig. One, a bearded man with a large purple scar on his forehead, black-pebble eyes and crane-like arms, crossed over to Sean's side and in accented English shouted, "Why you coming here? You belong on other side of the tracks."

"We're bringing milk to the school —" Sean began, but Bear cut him off.

"Beat it, Hebe," Bear ordered. "We're on official city business." He leaned forward and pointed to the SP badge and white armband on his shirt. "This means police," and, revealing the club, "this means I'm the boss."

"You are not the boss and not real police," hissed the second man. "You are scabs."

"Don't you call me a scab, you stinking Bolshevik!" Bear shot back, and stood up menacingly in the rig. "If I have to come down, I will rip out your eyeballs with my bare hands."

"Easy, Bear," Sean cautioned. "Let me handle this."

Without waiting for Bear's answer, Sean jumped down and motioned the bearded man to join him at the back of the rig. Pointing to the empty cans, Sean explained, "We're delivering milk to the schools so your families don't have to go without. See for yourself."

The man scrutinized the empty milk containers and turned back to Sean. "Okay, we let you pass."

After Sean jumped back up into the driver's side and grabbed the horse's reins, both men backed away from the rig and allowed it to continue.

"Stinking reds," Bear barked and spat. "You should've let me deal with them. The damn strike is making them think they can insult us. If it was up to me, they would all be shipped back to Bukovina or wherever the hell they came from."

The second incident occurred just past City Hall.

As they approached McDermot, four flat-capped men started walking parallel to the rig.

"Hey, how's it feel to be a couple of yellow-backed strikebreakers?" taunted one.

Sean ignored the insult.

"Why don't you get down off the rig and we'll show you what we do to scabs," threatened another.

"I've had enough," fumed Bear. "When I say *go*, speed up to McDermot, then stop the rig and get out with the club in your hand. Stand your ground and I'll charge them from behind."

"You're crazy!"

"Maybe, but I'm willing to bet these dimwits have never been in a real toe-to-toe fight. Ten to one they'll turn tail."

Seconds later Bear said *go* and slipped over the far side of the rig. As soon as it rapidly gained speed, the four strikers reacted exactly as he'd predicted and raced to keep up. By the time Sean stopped at McDermot, the strikers were almost at the rig. He pulled out the club, dismounted and faced them in a fighting stance.

The strikers stopped when they saw only Sean. "Hey, where's your goon pal?"

"Right here," said Bear from behind. "Now, what were you saying about showing us something?"

The closest man charged and took a wild swing, but Bear swerved and landed a blow on the side of his head. The man gasped in pain and crumpled to the sidewalk like a rag doll. Bear pivoted to face the next attacker, who was holding a knife. Smiling, Bear faced him with balled-fist hands. "C'mon, try me," he dared.

The man thrust at Bear. He sidestepped the movement and knocked the knife from his hand onto the sidewalk. It lay between them.

"Go ahead," Bear snarled. "But if I get to it first, I'll carve your face."

The striker retreated several steps, turned and ran.

One of the two men facing Sean lunged at him, but he brought the club up into the man's chin and knocked him reeling into the side of the rig. The remaining striker hesitated.

Sean moved aside, providing a clear path. "If I was you, I'd beat it. My partner's got your friend's knife and he's crazy."

The man looked over his shoulder at Bear, hesitated and then fled past Sean.

"Why did you let him go?" Bear asked angrily when he reached the rig.

"I had my fill of fighting in the war. That's it, plain and simple," Sean said defiantly. "Now, let's go!"

Bear confronts a striker.

Chapter 48
Winnipeg
The Strike — Day 30

Patterson couldn't get the scenes from the riot out of his mind. For the first time, he'd begun to actually worry about his safety — and apparently it wasn't just street violence he had to watch out for.

Am I really under surveillance? thought Patterson. *If so, who's trailing me? The RNWMP? Senator Robertson? Alfred Andrews?*

I need to find out.

Leaving the Alex, Patterson walked slowly down Main towards City Hall, scanning occasionally for a tail. He halted when he reached the Manitoba Hotel. Using the hotel's large front window as a mirror, he noticed a man in worker's clothes stopped across the street tying his shoelaces. Suspicious, Patterson reversed direction up Main, turned east at James and slipped into the first alleyway.

A minute later the same man passed by the alley.

Patterson needed a safe haven. His first thought was to return to the Alex, but he rejected this and, although he badly wanted a drink, dismissed the Criterion. Then it hit him! The Labour Temple was only a little further on James and the last place a tail would enter.

After fifteen minutes, he ventured from the alley, scanned up and down James and walked briskly to the Temple. Certain whoever had been trailing him was gone, he entered the building and asked the first person he met for Ivens.

"Downstairs."

Patterson found Ivens talking with a neatly dressed, stocky immigrant with a short neck, broad Slavic face and high peak of black hair. He looked to be in his forties.

When Ivens saw Patterson he waved him over. "Good morning. Nice to see you again. This is Mike Sokolowski."

Patterson greeted Sokolowski, who avoided eye contact and turned to Ivens. "I must go now. Thank you for help."

Once Sokolowski had left, Ivens explained, "Mr. Sokolowski is out of work, with a wife and three children. Too proud to let her use the Labour Café."

"I couldn't place his accent," stated Patterson.

"He's Ukrainian. There's a big community in the North End."

"What's he do?"

"Works in a metal factory as a tinsmith. All day he squats in fireboxes, hunches over blowtorches and crawls in and out of boilers."

"Dangerous work?"

"Indeed, not to mention bare wires and machines that can snatch his hair and poke his eyes."

"Are there warning signs?"

"Yes in *English*."

"Can he read English?"

"Not much," said Ivens. "Now, how can I help *you*?"

"I'm being followed."

"Followed?"

"Yes. A while ago someone tipped me off I was under surveillance. To be honest I didn't believe it. After all, I'm a reporter with a respected paper —"

"One that's sympathetic to workers," Ivens reminded him.

"—and have done nothing illegal during my time here."

"You've reported Senator Robertson believes the strike is an attempt at revolution."

"I was doing my job."

"Perhaps, but the authorities know you've spoken with me, as well as Russell, Dixon, Heaps and Helen Armstrong, *and* you've been seen at pro-strike returned-men's activities."

"That's true."

"I'm not sure what you're planning to do now, but no one would blame you for leaving if you feel under suspicion of committing a crime. By staying, you might in fact be risking your job and career."

"I don't plan on leaving," Patterson said stubbornly. "I still haven't found clear evidence that Robertson is colluding with the Citizens'."

"Hopefully you will," encouraged Ivens. "Now, *I* have a favour to ask you."

"How can I help?"

"My wife and I want you to come to dinner."

"Will accepting the invitation get me into even more trouble?"

"Perhaps."

To hell with it. "Of course I'll accept."

Leaving the Temple, he headed for the Criterion. He badly needed that drink, tail or no.

Chapter 49
Winnipeg
The Strike — Day 30

It took longer than expected, but eventually the RNWMP agent persuaded the Alex's manager to cooperate and provide Patterson's room key. Five minutes later he was in the room, where a search uncovered a battered typewriter, rough drafts and carbon copies of Patterson's *Advocate* dispatches. But no evidence of criminal activity.

However, the contents of the two-drawer chest revealed a small leather-bound book next to a half-empty bottle of whisky. Riffling the pages, he realized it was Patterson's diary. He pocketed it.

Stepping into the corridor, he noticed a chambermaid advancing up the hallway with an armload of fresh linen. He turned swiftly to face Patterson's door and pretended to be having trouble with the room key. To his relief she continued past, towards a service closet at the end of the hall. He walked calmly down the hallway and took the stairs to the lobby.

• • •

When Patterson returned to the Alex, he took the elevator up, not quite trusting his legs on the stairs.

"Good afternoon, Mr. Patterson," greeted the operator.

"Good afternoon," Patterson replied, making an effort not to slur.

"Too bad you missed your visitor."

"Visitor?"

"Yes, sir. The chambermaid observed a man outside your door. She reported the incident to me and I thought you might want to know."

"When did this happen?"

"Several hours ago."

"Thank you."

Patterson lurched down the hallway and stood unsteadily in front of his door. After digging out his room key, he fumbled then dropped it. Bending down to retrieve it, he nearly fell over. After several attempts he managed to place the key in the lock and open the door. He found nothing missing until he opened the chest of drawers. The bottle was still there, but his diary was gone.

"Jesus!" he exclaimed.

Can the entries prove anything illegal? Unlikely, but who knows for sure? Soon, however, fear was replaced by anger. How dare someone do this! No matter who it was, they had no right to steal his private property. *I've done nothing wrong and certainly nothing criminal.*

Chapter 50
Winnipeg
The Strike — Day 32

Patterson left the Alex, turned north at Main and Higgins and proceeded under the subway. His North End destination was Inkster Avenue. Once on the other side of the tracks, he continued on wooden sidewalks raised above the dirt-filled street. Passing a jumble of shoe shops, junk stores, barbershops, hardware stores and confectionaries, he met rag peddlers, tinkers, shoeshine boys and kerchiefed women. At Dufferin he wandered west for a block. On one side of the street were shops belonging to tanners, furriers, cobblers, jewellers and watchmakers; on the other were a bicycle repair store, steam bath, drugstore and tinsmith shop.

Backtracking to Main, he continued north and at Selkirk Avenue encountered the bazaar and bustling marketplace. Lingering among the street vendors and entertainers, he watched an old-fashioned hurdy-gurdy. Storefronts displayed piles of sprawling fish, tallow cakes, pot-bellied stoves, copper pots, brasses and bronzes, whipsaws, treadle sewing machines, spittoons, washboards and bustle dresses. Proof the area was home for Jewish immigrants were the many kosher poulterers, Shabbas fishmongers, challah bakeries, ritual slaughterhouses and shops selling prayer shawls. Men with side curls pushed fruit and vegetable carts, hawkers sold colourful trinkets and women wearing shawls and carrying black bags haggled with shop owners in Yiddish, Polish, Russian and Ukrainian.

As Patterson continued north on Main, a bewildering kaleidoscope of faces stared at him — men in skull caps and Roma-featured women. Down narrow dirt streets, back alleys and labyrinthine lanes, he saw poverty, misery and squalor. Outdoor privies substituted for indoor toilets, and backyard pumps and rain barrels replaced running water. Shoeless and ill-clothed children watched him with sorrowful eyes, and beggars implored him with outstretched arms and upturned palms. Feeling a mixture of pity and guilt for the inhabitants in the pathetic tenements, boarding houses and slums, he shuddered.

He turned west at Inkster and continued until he came to the Ivenses' neat two-storey wood-framed house on a narrow lot. On the screened verandah sat William and Louisa Ivens.

"Good afternoon," Patterson announced.

"Good afternoon," greeted Ivens. "I would like you to meet my wife Louisa."

"Hello, Mrs. Ivens."

"Pleased to meet you. My William has told me so much about how your reporting is helping the strike."

"Thank you."

"Please sit down," said Ivens. "We were just discussing the ongoing mass meetings in Victoria Park. A good friend of mine and fellow minister, James Woodsworth, intends to address the Labour Church in the park tomorrow night."

"I've heard a lot about Woodsworth and would like to meet him. What will he be saying?"

"He'll be talking about how the new Church must absolutely stand for education, inspiration and fraternity, Christ must be the greatest influence on people's lives, and with God's grace we must achieve a victory for workers here without violence."

Louisa went into the house and returned several minutes later. "Gentlemen, dinner is ready." They entered the modest

Patterson visits the North End.

dining room and sat down. "William," asked Louisa, "please say grace."

"For food in a world where many walk in hunger. For faith in a world where many walk in fear. For friends in a world where many walk alone. We give you thanks, O Lord. Amen," recited Ivens.

"Amen," said Louisa.

"Amen," added Patterson.

Dinner conversation inevitably focused on the walkout and the hardship it was causing strikers. Louisa feared working-class families were on the verge of collapse and women and children suffering terribly. With his chin resting on the tips of his steepled fingers, Ivens was strangely silent during the conversation. After the meal and cleanup, Louisa left the men alone.

"Mr. Patterson, I have a rather unusual and perhaps unpleasant request to help save lives, not souls."

Fifteen minutes later, and after thanking Louisa for the meal and her hospitality, Patterson said goodbye to her embattled husband. Standing beside him on the front steps, Patterson promised, "I will do my best with Senator Robertson, but what if he rejects your proposal?"

Ivens spread his hands and with a sorrowful expression on his face replied, "We all have to settle with the Lord one day, even the Minister of Labour."

Patterson said nothing and accepted a sealed letter. Hopefully Robertson would trust him as much as Ivens did.

Chapter 51
Winnipeg
The Strike — Day 32

Gideon Robertson waited impatiently in his second-floor luxury suite.

He had received a message from Patterson indicating he needed to deliver an urgent message from the Strike Committee. Robertson had agreed only to pursue his own objectives. Perhaps the meeting would provide an opportunity to raise the issue of Patterson's diary, or even warn him off further reporting.

A knock on the door announced Patterson's arrival. "Come in, please," said Robertson. He led Patterson into a room with several large vases, scarlet plush chairs and an eight-foot gilded mirror. On a mahogany side table were crystal glasses and a whisky decanter.

"I know you are very busy, Senator, and appreciate you seeing me on such short notice."

"Not at all. Would you care for a drink?"

". . . No, thank you."

"Very well. While I'm willing to listen to the Strike Committee's communication, I can make no promise of an official response."

"I understand your position completely. However, I want you to know I'm acting as a messenger for William Ivens and the Strike Committee, and not as a representative of the *Advocate*. Mr. Anderson wouldn't approve of my placing *his* paper in a position to ask a minister of the Crown a favour without his knowledge. In fact, I'm quite certain I would lose my job."

"Yes, indeed," Robertson acknowledged.

Patterson took a deep breath. "The Strike Committee wishes to end the walkout now, and if you accept their offer they will direct members to return to work in twenty-four hours."

Robertson gave him a skeptical look. "With all due respect, Mr. Patterson, I've heard this offer before from the Strike Committee. It's always conditional and with terms unacceptable to employers, the Citizens' and all levels of government."

"Perhaps, but I can assure you there are absolutely no conditions."

". . . How is this possible?"

"Permit me to explain. Up to this point the Strike Committee has insisted on three conditions to end the walkout: collective bargaining, wage increases and reinstatement of all workers."

Robertson nodded in agreement. Patterson continued, "Despite recent newspaper reports, the Committee has abandoned any hope the metal-trades employers will concede the issue of collective bargaining. As to wages, it's willing to accept a decision by the Manitoba Fair Wages Board. In this regard the Committee's hope is that Premier Norris can influence a just increase for workers in the metal trades and building-construction industries. On reinstatement of workers, the Committee will rely on the goodwill of all local employers and the various levels of government to take back workers who now voluntarily end the strike."

Patterson waited for Robertson to absorb the news. "To use a military term, the strike leaders are offering an unconditional surrender."

"I confess, this offer is most unexpected," Robertson admitted. "Why this sudden course of action?"

"First, the workers are running out of money. Most union members are broke, and sympathy strikers are even more desperate for wages simply to put food on the table and meet bills. The food kitchen at the Oxford Hotel can't help all those in need, and grocery stores are refusing worker families any more credit. As a result, some but not a significant number of strikers are returning to work."

Robertson said nothing.

"Second, there is ample proof violence is on the rise. The recent clashes involving returned soldiers, strikers and special police have already caused many injuries. As well, there are reports of a military-style buildup by General Ketchen at Minto and Osborne Barracks and by the RNWMP detachment. Unless the strike ends soon, the Committee feels there will be more injuries, and perhaps even deaths, on both sides. The strike leaders cannot condone violence and as you know have avowed this position from the start."

"Do you personally believe the Committee's offer is sincere?"

"Yes, or I wouldn't have risked my reputation and perhaps my job to come here tonight. Also, I have it in writing."

"In writing? Please let me see it."

Robertson arched his eyebrows as he read the offer signed by all fifteen members of the Strike Committee. "May I keep this? I need to confer with several people before making a decision."

"That isn't possible."

Robertson reluctantly returned the letter. "Do you wish to add anything more?"

"Yes."

"Please feel free to speak, on condition our conversation is still off the record."

"Certainly. I want to express how I feel about the authorities' handling of the strike. While I'm a firm believer in the British system of law and order and was raised to believe in monarch, empire and nation, since all levels of government have lined up against the strikers, it seems to me the workers are now also challenging the harmony of the British constitution. I believe the State must prevail, and it must do so to prevent the defeat of the British tradition of government."

"Well spoken, Mr. Patterson."

"However, I also remember the old teaching from school-days about British citizens having certain inalienable rights. Surely the workers in Winnipeg have the rights of assembly, association and speech."

"All British subjects have these rights, Mr. Patterson, and I too believe they should be preserved, but what is paramount in this situation is reconciliation of the strikers' rights and those of all citizens."

"Perhaps."

"Is there anything else you wish to add?"

"Yes. The use of special police may lead to government-sponsored violence."

Pausing, Robertson answered, "Hopefully not."

Patterson saw Robertson glance at this pocket watch. It was clear the meeting was over.

He must be under tremendous pressure, thought Patterson; *in fact, remaining in cabinet might depend on his successful settlement of the dispute.*

"I appreciate your consideration of the Strike Committee's offer."

"Goodnight, Mr. Patterson."

• • •

Robertson closed the door and sighed, "Too little too late, Mr. Patterson . . . too little too late."

Chapter 52
Winnipeg
The Strike — Day 32

Following the meeting with Patterson, Robertson was driven to RNWMP headquarters on Smith Street. Alfred Andrews was addressing the officers and special police.

"Tonight we will undertake an operation to arrest strike leaders and transport them to Stony Mountain prison. They will be remanded for eight days, denied bail and tried by a special immigration panel from Ottawa. Deportation is likely. Warrants will also be executed to search for and seize seditious literature in their homes, as well as in the Labour Temple, Ukrainian Labour Temple and Jewish Liberty Temple."

"Who will be arrested?" asked the senior RNWMP officer.

"Seven strike leaders and four foreigners."

"What are the charges?"

"All related to seditious conspiracy."

Andrews had eleven arrest and search warrants ready. He hesitated, however, when Robertson relayed news that the Strike Committee had proposed an end to the walkout.

"What are you going to do?' asked Robertson

"We have a spy in the Strike Committee and need to hear from him whether the strikers are really going to call off the strike."

After midnight word came.

At 2:00 a.m. police cars with armed officers swept down on the homes of the unsuspecting men.

Chapter 53
Winnipeg
The Strike — Day 33

Patterson awoke with a pounding headache. Following the meeting with Robertson, he had gone to the Criterion. *What will happen to the strikers?* he'd wondered. *What if Anderson learns about my unauthorized visit?* Trying to calm his swirling anxiety, he'd become so drunk he couldn't recall returning to the Alex. He woke still in his suit and shoes, collapsed sideways on his rumpled bed.

After a shower, a shave and a fresh change of clothes he made his way to the elevator.

"Good morning," announced the elevator operator. "Lobby, sir?"

"Please."

Three floors later, Davies squeezed into the elevator. His eyes met Patterson's. "Well, I guess you'll be heading back to Toronto now."

When Patterson blinked, Davies smirked. "Great news. The strike's sure to be over now. They say the devil gives the wicked more than their share of good luck."

"I've no idea what you're talking about."

"My God, you really don't know what has happened, do you? Looks like other papers will run this headline-grabber ahead of the *Advocate*. Patterson, you've been scooped."

Patterson's stomach flipped, his nausea no longer that of a hangover.

"C'mon Davies. What did I miss?"

"Last night several strike leaders were arrested and taken to Stony Mountain prison."

After a moment of stunned silence, Patterson's mind began to race. "Arrests? Who was arrested? By whom?"

"Calm down. Calm down," advised Davies. "Alfred Andrews, Senator Robertson and RNWMP officers, backed by specials, made the arrests. Robertson was out all night and returned to the hotel about four o'clock this morning with his bodyguard and four redcoats. Andrews arrived at four thirty. I was tipped off something like this was going to happen and staked out the lobby. When Robertson showed up I asked what was happening. He just smiled evasively and said, 'Nothing'."

"Wait a minute!" replied Patterson when the elevator stopped at the lobby. "Let me grab some details."

"Find out for yourself," rebuffed Davies. "In a poker game, winning isn't so much the luck of the draw as knowing how to read your opponents and then deciding when to call."

"What's your point?"

"The authorities now have put their cards on the table and are betting the arrests will end the strike."

"What do you think?"

"In my opinion the game's finally over. Now, if you don't mind, I have to go downtown and interview some people before I file my story."

Patterson now understood the look on Robertson's face at the end of their meeting — it was apprehension. He didn't want to reveal the impending arrests and allow a warning to strike leaders. Patterson wondered if showing Robertson the Strike Committee's offer had made him act even sooner.

Patterson exhaled. He had missed an opportunity for a scoop. *This can't happen again.*

The important thing now was to get a follow-up story.

Chapter 54
Winnipeg
The Strike — Day 33

In the early morning hours the strikers' headquarters presented a sorry spectacle. Glass windows on doors were broken, furniture smashed, a cigar stand looted and boxes of cigars that had eluded the authorities tossed aside. Offices were wrecked, papers, correspondence and file records seized, and supplies strewn on the floor. An axe had been used to break open doors, smash drawers and desks, and generally cause as much damage as possible.

A large crowd was milling about, including several local and out-of-town newspapermen, but there was no sign of the authorities or Strike Committee members. Recognizing a pro-strike returned soldier from Victoria Park, Patterson asked him who was arrested.

"I don't know. Ask that reporter over there."

"Which one?"

"The guy from the *Free Press*."

Patterson tapped Crandall on the shoulder. "Hi, Bob. I see events have attracted the press."

"Patterson! They sure have, but you're late to the show."

"I know. Can you fill me in?"

"Depends. What do you want to know?"

"Who was arrested?"

"Ivens, Russell, Heaps, Queen, Armstrong, Bray and four foreigners. They're still looking for William Pritchard."

"Who's he?"

"A Vancouver labour organizer."

"What are the charges?"

"Apparently related to seditious conspiracy. On separate warrants RNWMP officers searched homes and seized any concealed weapons and evidence of sedition. The Labour Temple, Ukrainian Labour Temple and Jewish Liberty Temple were also raided."

"What happened here?"

"According to eyewitnesses, the building was cordoned off by hundreds of specials and broken into by a dozen Mounties, who ransacked the offices of the Strike Committee."

"What about bail?"

"Don't know."

"Has the Strike Committee made any statement about ending the walkout?"

"Not yet."

"Where are the arrested men now?"

"In Stony Mountain Penitentiary."

"Where's that?"

"About ten miles north of the city."

"Thanks."

Just then, one of the city beat men shouted, "Look, there's Louisa Ivens, Helen Armstrong and Margaret Russell."

Patterson turned to see the women surrounded by a pack of reporters firing questions and scribbling down answers.

"Who is responsible for this outrage?" Louisa asked out loud. Upset but stoic, she recounted how a band of strange armed men broke into her home in the middle of the night and carried off her husband.

Someone asked if she had feared for their lives.

"Yes, because at first we thought they were intruders. Then my husband saw some were in uniform. But even so, they were just dreadful men."

"Did they harm you?"

"No, but they placed our children on the hard floor while they searched under the mattresses for 'seditious literature.' Imagine little children, half in fear and half in wonder, still in their nightclothes, forced to witness their poor father handcuffed and taken away in a waiting car."

"Did they say where your husband was being taken?" Patterson asked, after he had elbowed his way into the throng of reporters.

"No. Why would they take a Christian minister and treat him like a dangerous criminal? Is this Canada? Is this British law? Is this justice?"

"What happened at your place, Helen?" clamoured an American correspondent.

"One of them banged on the door and shouted 'Open up or I'll break it down'."

"What did you do?"

"I refused to let them in and insisted they couldn't take George until I called the police chief to prove the arrest and search warrants were legal. I made them wait while I ran to the closest police station and phoned the chief. Once he told me 'I guess it's all right,' I released George."

"What happened then?"

"While one redcoat stood at the back and a second at the front of the house, another searched every room, looking for incriminating letters, books and papers. There was one plainclothes man who really unnerved me because he didn't say a word, just stood poker-faced by the front door, calmly watching others do the dirty work. I could tell he was in charge. After ransacking the house and scaring our four children, they dragged George away and put him in a waiting car. The last thing he told me was to get hold of the WTLC's lawyer."

"What did they do at your place, Mrs. Russell?" asked a *Trib* reporter.

"They came to our house in Weston. It was in the small hours, about two in the morning. Our children were sleeping on the verandah when the Mounties burst into the house. One officer showed Bob the arrest and search warrant and in a while they were everywhere. I was not allowed to dress until the search was finished."

"Were you frightened?"

"Of course! I was in tears, but Bob told me not to worry. The last thing they did was handcuff him and shove him out the door and into a car."

Patterson was still writing when James Woodsworth came running up the street to the Labour Temple. Patterson let him catch his breath, then asked, "May I have your reaction to the arrests?"

Hopefully, Woodsworth's going on the record might persuade Anderson to forgive him for not being on top of the breaking news.

And at the very least, my version of the news will be a fair one.

Chapter 55
Winnipeg
The Strike — Day 33

By the end of the day Patterson learned Woodsworth and Fred Dixon had assumed direction of the *Labour News*. Their banner headline was *KEEP COOL — DO NOTHING: We've Got Them Beat Now*. Patterson added this information to his dispatch and raced to the GNWT office to wire the story before the paper's deadline for the evening edition.

• • •

The 800-word dispatch soon started coming in to the *Advocate's* telegraph operator.

By William Patterson
Special to The Advocate by Staff Correspondent
Copyright 1919, by The Toronto Advocate
Winnipeg, June 17

A sensation was sprung in Winnipeg at an early hour today, when men, who are supposed to be the leaders of the general strike movement, were arrested in the quiet of their homes by hundreds of mounted police and special constables. The arrested men include Reverend Wm. Ivens, editor of the Western Labour News, the strike paper, and

pastor of the Labour Church that has been
holding open air meetings in the parks on
Sunday nights; R.B. Russell, secretary of
the Metal Trades Council and an international officer, and credited with being one
of the dominating factors in the strike;
Alderman John Queen, advertising manager
of the Western Labour News, and member of
City Council for Ward Five; Alderman A.A.
Heaps, upholsterer, also a member of Ward
Five; R.E. Bray, one of the leaders of the
striking veterans; and George Armstrong,
a streetcar motorman, who was prominent
at the Calgary convention and has spoken
much during the strike at meetings in the
parks.

A warrant is also out for Vancouver labour
organizer William Pritchard. Four Rus-
sians were also taken into custody when
the arrests were made between two and four
a.m. this morning. All those arrested were
taken to Stony Mountain Penitentiary ten
miles north of Winnipeg.

Simultaneous with the arrests, the Labour
Temple, strikers' headquarters, was raided by the Royal North-West Mounted Police,
and literature seized. The building was
thoroughly searched and doors and rooms
that could not be opened were broken down.
Books and papers of all sorts were taken
and thrown into waiting automobiles. Also
raided were the Ukrainian Labour Temple
and Jewish Liberty Temple.

In an exclusive interview, James Woodsworth, who together with Labour MLA Fred Dixon has now assumed direction of the Western Labour News, reacted to the authorities' action. "The action is a stupid, high-handed move. Already the workers feel the government is not truly representative, that it represents only a section and not all the community." In response to whether the strike would now collapse, Woodsworth replied, "Not at all. The government can't arrest 35,000 strikers, and if the strike were broken the people still would insist upon handling their affairs and securing the ancient rights of Britons. There must be British justice. The arrested men have become martyrs to the cause of all workers. Yes, ten men have been arrested, but if necessary 100 more will take their place, and 100 more after that."

The Dominion Government is credited with orders to make all arrests. Senator Robertson, Minister of Labour, was out most of the night and returned to his hotel room about four this morning. Alfred Andrews, appointed Justice Department's representative in Winnipeg, was much in evidence last night.

After reading the lead and Patterson's interview with Woodsworth, Anderson handed the copy to the news editor. "Read the rest of the dispatch and see if editing is needed. If not, we'll run Patterson's story on the front page. I want the main headline in 72-point lettering: *Winnipeg Strike Leaders*

Are Arrested. Leftfield columns one and two will anchor the main story but will not be divided until after the lead. Let's slug-line the story *Ivens, Russell and Bray Now Held by the Police* until we find pictures of both Ivens and Russell. The remaining drop heads will highlight the police raids and the fact the Labour Temple, Ukrainian Labour Temple and Jewish Liberty Temple were broken into, searched and papers seized."

"Yes, sir. I suggest we run parts of the story as sidebar items in columns three and four. If necessary it will spill over to page two."

"Agreed," said Anderson. "While it's too late to include an editorial, I will prepare one for tomorrow titled *A Great State Trial.*"

As the editor turned to leave, Anderson commented, "I'm disappointed Patterson was late on news of the arrests and the raids, but his follow-up story is good. He better be on top of the next development."

Chapter 56
Stony Mountain Penitentiary
The Strike — Day 36

Bob Russell sat cold and sleep-starved in the gloomy silence of Stony Mountain Penitentiary. His nine-by-five damp cell had a toilet, sink and immovable bed covered by a thin mattress reeking of body odour, urine and tobacco. A single bulb in the ceiling covered by a wire cage provided barely enough light. After three days of solitary confinement, he had dark shadows under his eyes, was unshaven and wearing the same clothes from the night he was arrested.

"Get up, Russell. Someone's here to see you," demanded a guard.

"It's about bloody time this cutthroat business ended," Russell shot back, and set down his breakfast of milkless porridge, dry bread and black tea.

Two minutes later he was standing in front of Alfred Andrews.

With the prison warden as witness, Andrews read Russell's charge sheet.

You are formally charged with conspiracy to bring about a general strike, to endanger the lives of citizens and form illegal associations of employees, to break contracts, to establish a Soviet form of government in Canada and by reason of being a common nuisance during April, May and June 1919 endangering the life and property of citizens.

"I thought a man was supposed to go to jail after, not before, conviction?"

Ignoring the remark, Andrews replied, "Your deportation is going to be postponed until charges can be heard in court. You will be released tomorrow morning with bail on a personal bond of $2,000 and a pledge not to have any further direct or indirect involvement in the strike, including press interviews. Failure to comply will result in re-arrest."

"Who has authorized these conditions?"

"The federal government is allowing your release on grounds British justice would be best served by your temporary freedom and subsequent trial. The whole matter has been decided by officials in Ottawa."

"I suppose you and Robertson think your plan was brilliant, kidnapping men before their wives and children in the dead of night and keeping them hostage."

"Our actions were sanctioned by law, unlike yours, which have been deemed criminal. The citizens of Winnipeg have suffered unnecessarily for too long, and the authorities have determined you will face consequences for breaking the law."

"Arbitrarily arresting and imprisoning a British subject is illegal in this country. I have the right to be free from unreasonable search and seizure and being detained without due process."

"You will have your day in court, and a judge and jury will determine what is legal and just."

"Well, we'll see about justice, but meanwhile I can guarantee the strike will not end because of the Citizens' vendetta."

Chapter 57
Winnipeg
The Strike — Day 36

Bear and Sampson elbowed their way to the front through a swelling number of veterans in Market Square. An evening meeting would start soon to discuss what action to take about the arrests, Robertson's inability to settle the walkout, and the strike-breaking tactic of operating the streetcars.

"Quite the crowd," observed Sampson.

"Easier for Loyalists to go unnoticed," replied Bear.

"Now that Bray can't be involved anymore, who's going to address the men?"

"It doesn't matter. We're here to learn their plans."

Minutes later, the national anthem was announced, bringing men to their feet. As soon as the singing ended, Bray's replacement stood on a makeshift platform and raised his arms for quiet. "Men, if the Borden government won't settle this strike, then returned soldiers will."

To enthusiastic cheering, he continued, "Our veterans' committee worked all afternoon trying to reach a settlement. We've made an effort for weeks and the government has done nothing, so we won't stand for weak-stomached inaction any longer. Tomorrow afternoon at two thirty we will hold a monster silent indignation parade, which we believe is the most effective of weapons. No banners, songs, slogans or speeches. We'll simply march from City Hall to the Royal Alexandra Hotel and confront Senator Robertson."

"Looks like there'll be trouble tomorrow," whispered Sampson.

"It'll get nasty, but so what?"

"You're right, but do you really believe a march will force Robertson to settle the strike?"

"Not a chance, I —"

Before Bear could answer, the man next to them chirped, "Clam up, both of you. He's got more to say."

"Mass action is what we need now, with brains and brawn like we used in Flanders," Bray's replacement defiantly announced, stabbing the air with his forefinger. "I don't mean any rough stuff, though. If there are any barriers, keep calm and be silent. We want you to exercise restraint. Men, this isn't the time for broken heads."

His words were greeted with instantaneous applause and loud hurrahs. "Mr. Robertson is against the strike, and the government wants to starve the workers until the strike is beaten."

"Resign! Senator Strike-Breaker! Resign!" several returned men yelled, while others hissed at the mention of Robertson's name.

"Labour leaders have been arrested in their own homes in the middle of the night and their wives and children frightened."

"Shame! Disgrace!" responded even more voices, this time accompanied by loud hooting and booing.

"Is this the kind of democracy you men fought for in Belgium and France? Is it, men?"

"*No!*" came the thunderous reply.

"Then let's show solidarity tomorrow and force Robertson to end this strike, reinstate the railway clerks, policemen and postal employees, and stop the damned streetcars from running."

As whistles and applause filled the Square, he raised his arms and bowed his head to the crowd. The men rose to their feet, clapping continuously, until someone shouted, "Hip, hip, hurrah!"

"*Hip, hip, hurrah!*" came the much louder response. Finally, a third "HIP, HIP, HURRAH!" echoed deafeningly from all parts of the crowd, followed by a tiger.

Caught up in the moment, hundreds were soon on their feet. Bear and Ed also stood but didn't join the wild cheering. "We'll show them tomorrow, won't we?" a wide-eyed man beside Bear exclaimed.

"You bet we will!" sneered Bear as the mass of soldiers broke into "God Save Our Splendid Men."

• • •

Soon after news of the veterans' meeting at Market Square reached General Ketchen at Osborne Barracks, he sent an encrypted message to Ottawa.

```
PRO-STRIKE VETERANS PLAN TO MARCH TOMORROW -
STOP ESTIMATE SEVERAL THOUSAND - STOP WE ARE
PREPARED WITH MILITIA, SPECIAL POLICE AND
RNWMP TO ENSURE LAW AND ORDER - STOP
KETCHEN
```

Chapter 58
Bloody Saturday
June 21, 1919

Bear sat at the kitchen table carefully examining the Webley Mark VI he had taken off a dead British officer during the fighting in France. The double-action pistol with a fixed front post and rear notch sights was light and, with a short barrel, easy to carry. Holding the revolver in his left hand, he meticulously cleaned it with a chamois, then extracted the six rounds and burnished their nose tips to make a smooth flight to the next target. From experience Bear knew the Webley could fire twenty to thirty rounds and was most effective at close range. After lubricating and cleaning the revolver, Bear tested it in a well-worn ankle case that guaranteed concealment and no unwanted movement.

Leaving the holstered pistol on the table, Bear went into the bedroom and tenderly picked up the photograph of Jenny smiling proudly while holding a newborn Michael. After a few agonizing moments, he solemnly swore, "Jenny, I promise you, some Bolshevik bastard will pay dearly for what happened to you and our son."

After several hours of fitful sleep, Bear awoke gasping from a recurring nightmare. He was trapped in No Man's Land as shrapnel-laden shells burst all around. His rifle was just out of reach. He couldn't move his legs — they were tangled in a string of shattered barbwire. Jenny was running towards him, her arms outstretched, begging for help. Struggling was hopeless, as the wire held him firmly in its steely grip. Suddenly German machine guns opened fire. He screamed, *"Jenny, Jenny . . ."*

It was useless, as bullets ripped through her body. She threw her arms up and collapsed lifeless like a blood-soaked rag doll. All he could do was cry out, "No, no . . . no!"

His undershirt and shorts sweat-soaked and his whole body shaking, Bear pushed the images from his mind and stumbled to the bathroom. Breathing hard, he threw water on his face, only to see a broken man staring back in the mirror. Dragging himself back to bed, he lay staring sightlessly at the ceiling, until a persistent loud knocking on his door roused him.

"Bear, are you awake? We've been instructed to assemble at the Rupert Avenue police station in an hour and be ready for action when the silent parade takes place," came Sampson's excited voice.

Bear rolled out of bed, crossed the room and spoke through the door. "When do we see action?"

"We'll get our marching orders from the police chief once we're at the station. I've already talked to a few of the boys. They're real eager to give the reds a good licking today."

"I'll meet you there, Ed. I have to get dressed."

The last thing he did before leaving the apartment was to check and holster the Webley.

This is it, Jen. Time to get even.

Chapter 59
Bloody Saturday
June 21, 1919

Patterson awoke to the sound of a nearby gramophone. He recognized the song being played, "How Ya Gonna Keep 'Em Down on the Farm (After They've Seen Paree)?"

The first verse floated down the hallway:

How ya gonna keep 'em away from Broadway,
Jazzin' aroun', and paintin' the town?
How ya gonna keep 'em away from harm?
That's a mystery.

As the song continued, he imagined the windup Victrola with the large decorative horn and the record going around.

They'll never want to see a rake or plow,
And who the deuce can parlez-vous a cow?
How ya gonna keep 'em down on the farm,
After they've seen Paree?

It was ironic to hear the tune, because of its popularity with the soldiers overseas — the same men who were now the wild card in the strike.

Exiting the elevator, Patterson noticed Davies talking with Mayor Gray in the lobby. As soon as the exchange ended, he nabbed Davies.

"The mayor looks worried."

"Wrong," replied Davies. "He's plain scared. There's going to be trouble today and he's losing control of the situation."

"It's nine thirty. What's he doing in the hotel at this hour?"

Davies's eyes narrowed. For a moment Patterson thought he might walk away, but then he came to a decision and spoke.

"Why should I tell you?"

"You shouldn't," admitted Patterson.

"Damn right. But I've got an idea."

"What?"

"Since I can't be in two places at once, let's make a deal."

Not wanting to be scooped again, Patterson stared at Davies. "Looks like I have no choice."

"Serves you right. Here's the situation. Mayor Gray will be meeting in Robertson's suite in thirty minutes with Alfred Andrews, RNWMP Commissioner Perry and several pro-strike veterans." When Patterson said nothing, Davies added, "I used to work with a whisky drinker of incredible talent in Calgary, a mighty fine newspaperman. He once told me, 'Davies, don't ever meet trouble halfway, because it's quite capable of making the entire journey on its own'."

"I get it," said Patterson. "Robertson, Gray, Andrews and Perry are trying to head off today's silent parade by the returned men, aren't they?" When Davies nodded in agreement Patterson added, "That's what you meant about trouble and what the meeting is about, isn't it?"

"You bet, and if you want my opinion, it looks like everybody here and out on the streets is looking for trouble to meet them head-on."

"Where are you going now?"

"To City Hall. Word's out a bolstered RNWMP force, over 1,500 specials and 3,000 militia, are waiting for the order to stop the planned silent parade and break the back of the strike. With thousands of pro-strike returned soldiers on the streets, there's bound to be resistance against anybody stopping the march and operating the streetcars. My guess is when push comes to shove, there's going to be one hell of a barroom brawl this afternoon."

"What do you mean?"

"Jesus Christ, Patterson. *Do I have to draw you a picture?* The Mounties and the militia are armed to the teeth, and the specials are itching for payback for what happened to the mounted troop. Meanwhile pro-strike veterans are mad as hell and will force their march despite what the authorities say. Given these circumstances, a proper battle could take place."

Stabbing the air with his finger, he said, "Mark my words, somebody will get killed today! If you want a big story, safety will have to take a back seat to danger."

"What do you want me to do?"

"Get comments from anybody going to the meeting, then wait until I return."

"All right."

Before Davies scuttled out of the Alex, he handed Patterson a copy of the *Free Press*. "Read the mayor's latest proclamation." Patterson didn't have to look far. It was on the front page:

```
The proclamation issued by me some days
ago must be strictly adhered to. It has
been brought to my attention that a parade
of men, women and children is proposed for
today. I hereby reiterate my former procla-
mation that there shall be no parades until
the end of the strike. Any women taking
part in a parade do so at their own risk.
```

If the meeting couldn't result in a cancellation of the protest march, a full-scale riot was going to take place.

The clock was now ticking.

Chapter 60
Bloody Saturday
June 21, 1919

At 10:00 a.m. four returned men entered the hotel and went straight through the lobby to the elevator. Patterson raced up the stairs and intercepted them as they exited.

"William Patterson, *Toronto Advocate*," he said breathlessly. "Is there anything that can be done to prevent the silent parade?"

"End the strike," replied one of the veterans.

"And stop the damn streetcars!" said another.

Before he could ask another question, two uniformed RNWMP officers hustled the men into Robertson's suite. Jotting down the veterans' comments, Patterson returned to the lobby.

When Commissioner Perry and Andrews arrived, all Patterson could get out of Perry was *no comment*; Andrews said nothing and gave him a withering look.

At 1:00 p.m. a sweating and winded Davies returned. After catching his breath he asked, "What's been happening here?"

"It's hard to tell," replied Patterson. "The veterans are meeting with Gray, Robertson, Andrews and Perry, and a pair of Mounties are guarding the door."

"Is the meeting still going?"

"Yes."

"Christ, they've been in there for three hours. What's taking so long?"

"I don't know. What's it like downtown?"

"Unbelievable! Nobody seems to have a lick of sense anymore."

"What do you mean?"

"You wouldn't believe it. Thousands are milling near City Hall. Men, women and children, returned soldiers, strikers and their supporters, curiosity seekers, photographers, wire service and newspaper reporters. You'd think it was a national holiday, with people dressed in their best bib and tucker."

"What about the strike leaders?"

"Not one. I've heard they're keeping out of sight, though I did spot Helen Armstrong."

"See any Mounties?"

"None. Though it would be easy to have RNWMP plain-clothes men mix in the crowd."

"What about the specials?"

"Nope."

"That's odd. How about Ketchen's militia?"

"Couldn't see a single one."

"Perhaps the authorities have decided to allow the big parade and avoid a full-scale riot?"

"I don't think so."

"Why?"

"Because the streetcars are running."

"They are? Who's operating them?"

"Citizens' members."

"That's not going to sit well with the veterans. There'll be trouble if they use Main."

"Absolutely!"

"What about the parade?"

"If you ask me, I think it has about as much chance of reaching the Alex as a snowball in Hades, and *if* it leaves City Hall all hell will break loose."

"What are you going to do now?" Patterson asked.

"It's going to be a wild day, so I'm going to get a drink. Join me."

"No, thanks. Since missing the midnight arrests story, I'm off the booze."

Chapter 61
Bloody Saturday
June 21, 1919

"You shouldn't go to the parade," Amy Wells cautioned Helen Armstrong.

"George can't be there, but I can," replied Armstrong defiantly, "and I *will*."

"It might be dangerous. The mayor has warned that women who take part in the demonstration do so at their own risk."

"It's a scare tactic, Amy. We need to show the authorities and the Citizens' we aren't afraid."

". . . All right. I'll go with you."

"Bring a hat."

"Why?"

"You'll need the hatpin in case there's trouble."

They left the Labour Café and were soon in Market Square. Several strikers spotted and stopped Armstrong, firing questions about George. Wells drifted ahead. By the time she reached the small park in front of City Hall, she was alone.

The clock tower showed a quarter past one.

Chapter 62
Bloody Saturday
June 21, 1919

Sitting idle in the Rupert Avenue police station with Sampson and dozens of specials, Bear felt like a caged animal. It was 1:30 p.m., and with each passing minute the tension became more excruciating. Bear noticed almost everybody was armed. Most had wooden clubs, but a few sported billies, brass knuckles or loaded hosepipes. One special had a foot-long chain covered in leather with a short heavy clevis and bolt attached to the end.

No one knew Bear was carrying the Webley.

After receiving instructions to deal with the anticipated confrontation near City Hall, several specials who knew that Bear had fought overseas asked his advice. He made it clear how they should proceed.

"In combat the ideal situation is to surprise a target, whereupon you can converge from all sides and then destroy it. That's exactly what we need to do today."

"God, this could be a bloodbath," groaned a young special.

"I didn't sign up to get hurt," chimed in another.

"Some of you have experienced close-quarters fighting," Bear pushed back, "and know it's brutal and bloody. Today's no different. Just consider them targets."

"But they have us outnumbered, Bear!" exclaimed Sampson.

"They may have the numbers, but with courage we'll succeed, just like we did at Passchendaele."

Sampson nodded in agreement, but Bear could tell a few were still unconvinced, so he tore into them. "Quit moaning. Stiffen your spine and don't stay if you feel sorry for yourself or them. They sure as hell have it coming."

Chapter 63
Bloody Saturday
June 21, 1919

After returning from the Ukrainian Labour Temple to find his wife, Mike Sokolowski was told by a neighbour she had taken their children to the strikers' food kitchen. Furious, he stormed out of the dingy tenement and headed to the Oxford Hotel. At Main and Rupert he was passed by a virtually empty streetcar making its way north to Higgins. *Why are the streetcars running?* The strikers would never let them operate unless the walkout was over.

Was it?

Once Sokolowski reached City Hall, he could go no further than the Manitoba Hotel. The sidewalks were choked with men in dark suits and white straw hats, felt fedoras and soft cloth caps, and women wearing wide-brimmed hats and skirts with hems brushing the street. Adding to the congestion, a great stream of automobiles was passing up and down Main.

"What is happening?" he asked a young man in uniform.

"We're going to have a parade."

"We?"

"Returned soldiers."

"Is strike over?"

"No."

"But streetcar pass me."

"Yeah. Operated by scabs. We pulled the trolley off the lines several times, but it forced its way through us. We'll stop the next one."

Chapter 64
Bloody Saturday
June 21, 1919

"Law and order must be maintained," insisted Mayor Gray.

"That is exactly why we want the streetcars stopped," said the oldest veteran. "Operating them is a strike-breaking tactic which will lead to *disorder*."

"The citizens of this city are entitled to this service," Gray responded as calmly as possible.

"And if the strike isn't settled by two o'clock, we'll hold the parade."

"The authorities have absolutely committed to the breaking up of any demonstrations," explained Gray. "You have ignored my proclamations, not once but twice, and threaten to do so a third time. The parade will be stopped, peacefully if possible, but if not, other means will have to be taken."

"Well, if you can't meet our demands, you should resign."

"I will do no such thing!"

At 1:45 p.m., the police chief phoned with more bad news.

"I'm sorry to break into your meeting, Your Worship, but the crowds outside City Hall and down Main as far as Portage are huge and getting bigger by the minute. The situation is out of control."

"Can't the specials handle things?"

"It's not possible. The silent parade is set to start in forty-five minutes, and the crowd numbers in the thousands. I strongly urge you to return to City Hall."

"I'm on my way," Gray finally agreed.

"Thank you," said a relieved chief, and added, "Take a back street because Main is jammed starting at James."

"Fine."

"Any further orders, sir?"

"No. Wait until I assess the situation."

Returning to the meeting, Gray interrupted the conversation. "My apologies, gentlemen, but events at City Hall require my immediate attention. Commissioner Perry, may I have a word with you privately?"

Perry joined Gray in the hallway.

"The police chief has informed me there's a large crowd massed in the vicinity of City Hall. I may need your men to help the special police enforce the ban on public meetings. This parade must be stopped!"

"Certainly. My men are at your disposal."

"How large a force do you have?"

"Fifty-four mounted officers and two dozen more in trucks."

"I'll contact you if necessary."

Gray drove down King Street to City Hall, where he was met by the police chief at the rear entrance. They rushed through the building and out onto the front steps. From the parapet Gray saw a seething mass of people filling Main and spilling over onto William and Market. The atmosphere was charged, the noise overwhelming. The crowd seemed like some dark prehistoric beast, growling and ready to strike.

Gray was shaken. Realizing the specials could never handle the situation once the parade started, he retreated inside City Hall and, in the presence of the police chief, phoned Perry.

After the call, he turned to the chief. "Get me the Riot Act."

Chapter 65
Bloody Saturday
June 21, 1919

At 2:10 p.m. the veterans stormed out of Robertson's suite. Patterson buttonholed them for a comment.

"Our plans are not defined," stated the oldest ex-serviceman.

"What do you mean?"

"The authorities have forbidden today's planned silent parade and have threatened direct action against any demonstrators, so we're trying to find an alternative place to peaceably assemble."

"What about the streetcars?"

"They have refused to stop operating them."

"What's going to happen?"

He didn't answer, but remained huddled in a heated discussion with the others. Abruptly two left.

"Where are they going?" Patterson asked.

"With Alfred Andrews in his automobile to try and arrange for the men to meet in the Convention Hall at the Industrial Bureau."

"Where's Mayor Gray?"

"He left the meeting after a telephone call from the police chief."

Seeing Robertson across the lobby, Patterson broke off from the returned men. Barely constraining his anger at Robertson's deceit about the strike leaders' arrests, Patterson realized if he wanted answers now, he would have to avoid bringing up their last conversation.

"Senator Robertson, can you tell me what's happening?"

"My offer to speak to the marchers at Victoria Park has been rejected," was his curt reply.

"Why?"

"Unfortunately I cannot announce a strike settlement."

"What about the silent parade?"

"Mayor Gray has reiterated the ban on demonstrations," Robertson replied evasively, "and he has told the veterans any women who are in the vicinity are there at their own risk. Now I must be on my way."

Patterson blocked his path. "If the parade does go ahead, what will the authorities do?"

Robertson did not answer, but his RNWMP bodyguard moved in between them.

"Do you expect civil unrest today?" Patterson shouted as Robertson began to walk away.

Robertson turned. "Mr. Patterson, be careful. If you fear for your safety, stay away from the parade."

Patterson jotted down Robertson's comments. *No way I am staying here.* Leaving the Alex, he raced down Main. *I'm way past being careful.*

By the time Patterson passed James, both sides of Main were fronted fifteen deep. Squeezing into the entranceway of a building near the Manitoba Hotel, he positioned himself to see down Main and across to City Hall. Although a photographer was taking shots from the third floor of the Union Bank building and several newspapermen were watching safely from the roof of the Pantages Theatre, Patterson made a fateful decision.

He would remain at street level.

Chapter 66
Bloody Saturday
June 21, 1919

With the town clock at half past two, word passed among hundreds of pro-strike returned men gathered on each side of the tracks to *fall in*. At the same time, Patterson noticed Portage Avenue streetcar Number 596 approaching Market Street from the north. Prevented from going any further by a large crowd, the half-full tram was greeted by a roar of booing, and its trolley was pulled off the line. Strap-hangers inside fled and dispersed among the crowd; the conductor and motorman quickly abandoned their posts.

As the angry crowd surged around the now empty streetcar, Patterson heard those closest shouting, "Tip it over! Tip it over!"

Soon, dozens began rocking the streetcar. When it proved too heavy to topple, two men clambered inside. While one smashed windows, the other slashed several seats and set them on fire.

As dark clouds of smoke billowed into the air above the streetcar, someone yelled, *"Here come the bloody soldiers!"*

Patterson ran out onto the street, craning his neck to see above the crowd. Advancing towards the streetcar was a single line of red-coated RNWMP riders, followed closely by a line of khaki-clad horsemen and a convoy of trucks, rounding the corner of Main from the south, opposite the Union Bank building. As the line of horsemen quickened their pace, they swept Main from gutter to gutter. The crowd opened up, letting the Mounties pass around the burning streetcar, then closed in and pelted them from behind with bricks and bottles.

The riders continued several blocks north, regrouped and returned down Main. Patterson watched two columns of four, on each side of the street, drive the missile-throwers back onto the sidewalks with their truncheons. By the time the troop reached the Union Bank building, two horses were riderless.

The crowd tips a streetcar.

Chapter 67
Bloody Saturday
June 21, 1919

As smoke billowed from the derailed streetcar, Mayor Gray appeared on the parapet of City Hall. Amidst the noise and confusion, he began reading the Riot Act.

"His Majesty the King charges and commands persons being assembled," Gray shouted over the din, *"immediately to disperse peaceably to depart to their habitations or their lawful businesses, on the pain of being guilty of an offence for which, on conviction, they may be sentenced to an imprisonment for life."*

As he finished with "God Save the King," the minute hand of the clock tower ticked to two thirty five and a crackle of gunshots pierced the air. Several demonstrators charged the steps, attempting to pull Gray down off the stone ledge and onto the steps, but he retreated into City Hall. Quickly leaving the building, he drove to Osborne Barracks and requested Ketchen to assemble all available militia.

Chapter 68
Bloody Saturday
June 21, 1919

When the shooting started, ex-servicemen instinctively dropped for cover; others panicked and streamed like quicksilver into nearby courts and alleys.

Patterson stood transfixed.

"Get on the ground! They're shooting with real bullets!" screamed a returned man. Patterson hit the ground and looked up to see several scarlet-clad riders wheeling towards him with unholstered Colt .45 revolvers in one hand and clubs in the other. They fired a volley, muzzles flashing.

Ejected shell casings bounced with a loud *ping* on the street. When the smoke cleared, those remaining on the sidewalks and in the streets retaliated with stones and bottles. Despite the barrage, the Mounties unleashed another fusillade, this time directed towards the burning streetcar.

Firing continued until the Mounties had emptied their Colt .45's, the final hail of bullets striking people, pockmarking buildings and ricocheting off the pavement and cobblestones like balls in a pinball machine. In front of the burning streetcar, a mother threw her arms protectively around her little boy and dashed across the street for shelter in the trees fronting City Hall.

Chapter 69
Bloody Saturday
June 21, 1919

A man next to Wells had been nicked by a bullet. He tottered against a brick wall as the woman with him screamed for help. Several other blood-stained figures lay wounded on the smoke-filled streets; a bystander who had been shot in both legs lay moaning on the sidewalk in front of the Union Bank building.

One of the red-coated officers, knocked off his horse by a rock, lay on the streetcar tracks. His long, leather-thong truncheon had been stripped by a striker, who was giving him a terrific beating. A second injured redcoat was being dragged across Main to the doorsteps of a funeral parlour.

Wells then saw something she would never forget. While crossing the street in front of the Manitoba Hotel, a man was struck in the chest by a bullet. He spun around like a top and slumped to the pavement. A striker next to him quickly dropped the rock in his hand, which he had been about to throw at the Mountie, and fled. The officer's bullet had missed the rock-thrower and hit a bystander.

Wells shouted for help, but no one came.

RNWMP officer shoots Mike Sokolowski.

Chapter 70
Bloody Saturday
June 21, 1919

Patterson saw the man collapse in front of the Manitoba Hotel and was certain death had come instantly. Despite the continuing hail of bullets, including one round that sped past his shoulder, he ran across the street and skidded on his knees next to the fallen body. He pulled aside the man's shirt collar and checked his carotid artery. The skin was still warm, but there was no pulse.

Patterson pulled out the man's wallet and removed an alien-registration card and family photograph. *Mike Sokolowski, tinsmith, of 552 Henry Avenue*, indicated the card. The photograph showed a nondescript, peasant-faced woman with three small children. Was he the same Sokolowski from the Labour Temple, Patterson wondered. He lifted and turned the man's head. It was him!

He closed Sokolowski's eyes.

Patterson felt tears start in his own eyes, but he realized the man's death presented a golden opportunity. *A scoop!* He stuffed Sokolowski's wallet into his own pocket. *I have to get to the GNWT office. Now!*

Chapter 71
Bloody Saturday
June 21, 1919

Once shots were fired, armed specials swarmed out of the Rupert police station like angry hornets. While most headed to Main to cordon off the thoroughfare near City Hall, smaller contingents were sent to intercept demonstrators fleeing down backstreets and alleys.

Patterson was hit with a wave of indecision. Things were about to get even uglier. *I can either cover the rest of the riot, or wire the scoop.* He decided to stay. Who knew what else could happen? The scoop would have to wait.

Seeing specials manhandling several men near the smoldering streetcar, Patterson ran down a nearby alley for a temporary hiding place — only to discover it was a dead end. Moments later he heard shouting from the alley's mouth and saw two men with white armbands and clubs enter. Their voices echoed, intensifying in the narrow space, as they started down towards him.

Breathing hard and trying to control his shaking hands, Patterson froze in the shadows, his back to the wall. *God help me!*

Terrified, he heard the specials come closer. When they were a few steps away, he emerged with his hands over his head, shouting, "I'm a reporter! I'm a reporter!"

"Face the damned wall! Arms out and spread your legs,

you son of a bitch!" snarled the taller of the two. "I'm going to pat you down. One false move and I'll crack open your skull." While he roughly frisked Patterson, his partner scrutinized the *Advocate* press credentials. "He's clean. No need to cuff him," announced the special and roughly spun Patterson around.

"His identification is good," confirmed his partner. "Let him go."

"You're lucky, pal," spat the special holding him up against the wall. "Now get the hell out of here."

Sweat-soaked and gasping, Patterson slumped down the wall and was violently sick in the gutter. He tried to stand, but his body refused to obey the order from his brain. It took a few minutes for his heart to stop hammering and chest to stop heaving. He had been lucky. His press card had saved him a beating and arrest. Possibly his life.

Standing unsteadily, he noticed something at his feet. It was one of the specials' armbands. He slipped it over his arm.

Leaving the alley, Patterson came upon men, women and children running away from Main. In pursuit were dozens of specials.

Among the fleeing mob, he caught a glimpse of gleaming red hair.

Patterson joined the charge.

Chapter 72
Bloody Saturday
June 21, 1919

After the firing stopped, a striker next to Wells shouted in broken English, "Look. Specials come! We must go!"

"Where to?" she implored.

Pointing to a large group of men and women escaping down a side street, he said, "We follow them!"

As Wells caught up to the escaping throng, it veered down a long, narrow alley towards Victoria Park.

Not far behind were the specials.

Wells entered the alley and noticed both sides were the back ends of brick warehouses. The buildings were so closely abutted there were no passageways in between, and while there was a latticework of narrow, rear-mounted fire escapes, their bottom rungs were unreachable from ground level.

The alley felt like a tunnel.

"Watch footing!" the striker warned, pointing to half-buried tracks from an old rail spur.

Midway up the alley, those in front of the fleeing crowd suddenly stopped.

"Why has everybody —"

"Specials!" someone yelled. "They've blocked the exit."

She wheeled. More specials were blocking the entrance from where they'd come.

Chapter 73
Bloody Saturday
June 21, 1919

Spoiling for a fight, Bear and Sampson stood at the entrance to the alley. At the other end were more specials. In between were dozens of men and women. Trapped like fish in a barrel.

The specials didn't immediately charge. Instead, in an intimidating gesture, they tapped the cobblestones with the bottoms of their clubs, at first lightly, then louder and faster, like a drumbeat.

• • •

Patterson caught up to the specials blocking the alley's entrance and pushed his way to the front row. He was certain Wells was in the trap.

I didn't fight in the war and I've never done anything heroic. Time to prove myself.

Chapter 74
Bloody Saturday
June 21, 1919

What happened next, in what became known as Hell's Alley, took less than ten minutes.

The specials' tapping petered into ominous silence.

Bear threw back his shoulders. "Now, boys. Let's give it to them damn reds!"

Some caught in the full-on assault searched for anything to throw at the advancing specials, but few missiles were available; others pulled out their belt buckles. Most attackers and defenders alike squared off in hand-to-hand combat.

Bear and Sampson cornered a flat-capped striker beneath a fire escape ladder, the bottom of which was just too high for him to reach, though he tried desperately to grab it. While Bear and Sampson had clubs, the striker had only fists. As he brought up his arm to fend off Sampson's blow, Bear viciously swung his club and connected with the man's jaw. Several teeth cracked and splintered. Screaming in pain, the striker crumpled to the ground.

• • •

"Amy . . . *Amy!*" shouted Patterson.

He found her halfway down the alley — sitting in the gutter, her arms wrapped about bent, mud-smeared knees. Rocking back and forth, she was crying uncontrollably. Her right forearm was bleeding, and the side of her face was bruised and swollen.

"I try protect her," protested the striker who was crouched next to her, "but they knock me down." The man was sporting an ugly black eye and looked like he was missing several teeth.

"It's not your fault," said Patterson, and threw his arms around the sobbing woman's shoulders.

She recoiled at this touch. "Please don't hit me again. Please don't hit —"

"It's Will, Amy. Don't worry. You're safe now."

Chapter 75
Bloody Saturday
June 21, 1919

Bear stepped in front of Patterson, the red-haired woman and the striker. Patting his club menacingly, he sneered. "Now it's your turn, pal!"

He swung the club but misjudged the man's speed and received a well-aimed kick in the groin. Doubling over, Bear dropped the club and fell to the ground. On his knees, he reached down, unsnapped his ankle holster and pulled out the Webley.

Pointing the gun at the striker, he shouted, "You Bolshevik bastard! You're going to pay for Jenny and Michael."

"Bear, no!" Patterson cried.

"Please. No shoot!" begged the striker.

Ignoring the man's plea, Bear pulled back the hammer and fired. The Webley went off with a deafening bang.

• • •

Patterson reached Bear seconds before he pulled the trigger. Hitting his arm at the elbow, it was just enough to cause the Webley's muzzle to tilt upwards when it fired. The bullet cracked dangerously close to Wells's head and into the brick wall.

Head ringing with the sound of gunfire, Patterson knocked the revolver from Bear's grasp. It fell to the ground. Bear reached for the gun, but Patterson shoved him aside.

"I've got it!"

Taking Wells by the arm with one hand and pointing the revolver with the other, Patterson and the striker led her out of the alley.

Patterson struggles with Bear in Hell's Alley.

Chapter 76
Bloody Saturday
June 21, 1919

They reached the General Hospital to find it overflowing with injured men and women, many with gunshot wounds. A triage nurse told Patterson Wells's injuries weren't serious, and it would be some time before she could be treated.

"Thank you, Will," said Wells gratefully, reaching out to touch Patterson's hand. "I'll be fine. Go. You have a job to do. Tell the world what happened here today."

"Are you sure?"

"Yes. You're a good man, Will Patterson. I'll never forget you."

"Perhaps we'll meet again," he said affectionately, knowing it might be the last time.

"I would like that."

Chapter 77
Bloody Saturday
June 21, 1919

Even with his press credentials, it took Patterson more than
an hour to clear the specials' roadblocks, dismounted
RNWMP and Ketchen's militia on his way to the GNWT office.
There he dictated the Sokolowski scoop and a detailed story
of the riot to the Morse operator, who hammered it out line
by line to the *Advocate*.

On his way back to the Alex, he stopped at the Rupert
Street jail and asked for the police chief.

"What do you want?" barked the embattled officer.

"My name is William Patterson. I'm a reporter with the
Toronto Advocate. Here's the identification card for the man
shot dead in front of City Hall."

"How did you get this?"

"I took it off him."

"You could be arrested for doing that."

"I would be fired if I didn't."

"Don't be a smartass."

Patterson held his breath then let it out in a gust. "One
more thing. There's a special nicknamed Bear."

"I know who he is," the chief replied.

"He tried to shoot someone during the riot."

"How do you know this?"

"Here's his gun," said Patterson, and handed over the

Webley.

"How did you get this?"

"I knocked it out of his hand during a struggle."

"Any witnesses?"

"Yes. Myself and a young woman."

The chief examined the Webley. Noticing the missing round, he looked at Patterson. "You may need to make a statement. How can I reach you?"

"I'm staying at the Royal Alex."

"All right. I'll take care of this."

"Be careful. Bear doesn't seem in his right mind."

"Most likely from shell shock during combat."

"A nervous breakdown?"

"Exactly."

"What are you going to do?"

"I'm going to hold him at Tuxedo Hospital. There's a doctor there who specializes in vets with this condition. I'll see Bear gets treatment."

"How long will he be held there?"

"Until he recovers."

Chapter 78
Winnipeg
The Strike — Day 38

The exclusive, all-male Manitoba Club of the city's Anglo-Saxon elite was located on Broadway, in between the Fort Garry Hotel and the Canadian National Railway station. Two Citizens' executive members entered the building together, climbed the impressive interior oak staircase and were soon relaxing in a private room.

"Let's have a celebratory drink," said the President.

"A good idea," replied Alfred Andrews.

Over the club's best brandy and cigars, the President spoke first. "You don't seem at all troubled by yesterday's events."

"Why should I?" Andrews remarked. "I gave the returned men an opportunity to meet before the parade at the Industrial Bureau, but they refused. The mayor warned all citizens not to assemble, and once he read the Riot Act, force was legally necessary to ensure law and order and prevent civil insurrection."

"You're right, of course. Now it's time to get back to business as usual."

"I agree we need normalcy, but this whole affair isn't over yet by a long shot."

"What do you mean?"

"I intend to use the courts to criminally prosecute the strike leaders, starting with Russell. I'm going to teach him and the others a lesson they'll never forget."

"What's that?"

"We control this city."

Chapter 79
Winnipeg
The Strike — Day 39

Ivens opened the door on Patterson's second knock.

"Hello, Mr. Patterson," he whispered. "Come in, but please be quiet. Our little boy has been unwell for two days and Louisa is very concerned because he doesn't have a strong constitution."

"I'm very sorry to hear about his health," sympathized Patterson as he studied the worried expression on Ivens's face. "Everyone knows you and your wife have already had enough trouble lately."

"Thank you. What can I do for you?"

"Is it true the walkout will end tomorrow?"

"The best person to answer that is Bob Russell. He's here."

Patterson blinked in surprise and followed as Ivens led him to the kitchen.

"Hello, Mr. Russell."

"Good morning, Patterson."

"Has the Strike Committee decided to end the walkout?"

"Yes. Most working-class families are starving, WTLC strike funds are exhausted and the authorities are absolutely determined to crush the walkout. Given the upcoming trials of the arrested strike leaders, it's also evident the government intends to publicly humiliate and then punish those of us who played a prominent role in organizing and leading the walkout."

"Can the Strike Committee give rank-and-file members any positive results of the walkout?"

"Not really, unless you consider Norris ordering a provincial investigation into the strike."

"Will the labour movement in Winnipeg be seriously wounded by the strike's collapse?"

"Let me answer that," volunteered Ivens. "Jesus suffered wounds too."

Patterson hesitated to ask the next question, but Ivens seemed to read his mind. "You want to know if I think I'll go to jail."

"Yes."

"I don't know. Although the strike leadership did have a common goal to improve the lot of the workers and once the walkout was underway we agreed to a policy of peaceful idleness, I can truthfully testify there was no conspiracy among those of us who've been arrested. If we're guilty of anything, it's naiveté, not revolution. However, despite our innocence, I do believe the Citizens', led by Alfred Andrews, will prove otherwise in a court of law. As Plato said, *Power corrupts, and absolute power corrupts absolutely.* Should that be the case and I'm found guilty by a jury of my peers, I'll accept imprisonment as a result of blind justice and perhaps, as Dafoe has predicted in the *Free Press*, become a martyr for the working class."

Turning to Russell, Patterson said, "How do you feel about ending the strike?"

"Tell your readers we'll live to fight another day. What has happened here is not just a strike but a larger fight for workers' rights that won't be easily broken."

They talked for a few minutes and then shook hands. "Be careful," cautioned Russell. "You've become personally involved in the strike. There's a good chance you'll be arrested too."

"I plan to stay."

"No," insisted Russell. "You have to go back to Toronto as soon as possible. We need you to get out the truth."

Chapter 80
Winnipeg
The Strike — Day 40

As usual, Anderson's telegram was brief.

STRONG BLOODY SATURDAY COVERAGE - STOP
CONGRATULATIONS ON THE SOKOLOWSKI SCOOP -
STOP WRAP UP WITH AN EXPOSURE - STOP
ANDERSON

Patterson returned to his room, thought-heavy. *What can I expose without being arrested?*

A knock on the door interrupted his thoughts.

"May I come in?" Davies announced in his gravelly voice.

"I'm busy," lied Patterson.

"Won't take a minute. It's important."

"All right, come in."

"I heard through the grapevine you might be leaving us."

"I may be recalled to Toronto and reassigned."

"Well, now that's a shame, because this strike business isn't over yet, not by a long shot."

"You mean the trials?"

"Exactly! There's sure to be another big story around the trials, and I'm hoping you'll be here to cover them."

Ignoring Davies's taunt, Patterson said, "Do you believe those arrested will go to trial?"

"My God, yes!" he blustered. "As they say back in the Kentucky mountains, 'Some days you eat the bear, and some days the bear eats you'."

"What do you predict the verdict will be?"

His florid face beaming, Davies laughed out loud. "An open-and-shut case. Alfred Andrews will ensure a guilty charge for the whole damned bunch. I say put 'em in the lockup and throw away the key."

It was a bittersweet moment for Patterson. How sad, that Davies and his kind couldn't admit they were wrong about the true goals of the strike leaders. *How many other fights will there have to be, to achieve fairness for the working class?*

Patterson then shook Davies's outstretched hand and solemnly stated, "If the final verdict sends them to prison, I can assure you the law and justice will be two entirely different things."

Chapter 81
Winnipeg
The Strike — Day 40

After Davies left, the exposure Anderson wanted suddenly came to him. It would be about the man who, from the start to the finish of the strike, was everywhere without anyone noticing.

Two hours later he ripped the last sheet out of the Underwood.

Andrews the Brains of Strike Opponents

By William Patterson Special to The Advocate
by Staff Correspondent
Copyright 1919 by The Toronto Advocate

If R.B. Russell, the Socialist machinist was the outstanding leader of the Winnipeg general strike, Alfred Andrews, K.C., was the principal factor in opposing the strike movement. Those two men were generals directing the strategy of opposing forces. Unlike in age, appearance, training and ideals, they were not unequal rivals. Andrews himself would be the first to admit that Russell is well-posted as to economics and labour organization and a man of more than ordinary native ability. The battle between these two clever tacticians provided a fascinating study apart from the magnitude of the national issue involved.

Russell was not worsted until Andrews was given the opportunity to use the powers of the State to put Russell in custody and eliminate him as a factor in the strike. Andrews is old enough to be Russell's father. His hair, long in the front and rather thin, is iron grey and often tousled. His face is clean shaven, with a pipe usually in the mouth. He is not at all finicky about his clothes and general appearance. Andrews often was seen during the strike, with a wilted collar dashing about the city.

He was here, there and everywhere, directing the operations of the Citizens' Committee of One Thousand, as a member of the executive, finding and assembling evidence against the strike leaders, as a representative of the Justice Department drawing up charges, directing raids, supervising arrests and holding innumerable conferences with authorities, business and labour leaders.

It is an open secret that the Citizens' Committee dictated nearly every move made against the strike by the City Council. Council readily followed intimations that the police force should be dismissed, pledges against sympathetic strikes be exacted from all civic employees, various

```
public   utilities   be   operated   by  volun-
teers,  a  monster  force  of  special  police
be recruited at six dollars a day, and ice,
and milk be distributed from the schools.

Probably no one person had more to do with
these various moves than had Mr. Andrews.
He is credited with having had a hand in
framing the change in the Immigration Act
rushed through Parliament in one hour,
which would permit British-born agitators
to be deported after summary trial, and
he certainly was responsible for the sen-
sational round-up of the strike leaders
and their imprisonment in a penitentiary
ten miles from the city. Enlistment of a
large citizen army, use of Royal North
West Mounted Police, forcing the railway
company to operate the streetcars, are all
moves supposed to have been made after
Andrews had voiced his approval.
```

After Anderson read Patterson's story, he called in his news editor and handed it to him. "Tell me what you think."

"This is excellent."

"I agree. Patterson's come a long way since he first showed up, insecure but eager to prove himself. This story about Andrews is almost as sensational as the Sokolowski scoop. Patterson has been making history with his reporting, hasn't he?"

"Yes, sir. Is it time to bring him home?"

"Indeed it is."

Chapter 82
Winnipeg
The Strike — Day 42

Patterson waited on a platform bench for the evening CPR train to Toronto. He had serious misgivings about leaving, including a desire to continue reporting the strike and leaving people he had come to respect — Ivens, Russell and Helen Armstrong. *Amy Wells.*

Patterson felt a tap on his shoulder. He turned to see a well-groomed and rugged-looking man of about thirty looking at him with steely cold eyes. The man discreetly revealed an identification card belonging to RNWMP *Sergeant Dawson*.

"Senator Robertson wishes a few minutes of your time before you catch your train," the officer announced. When Patterson hesitated, he felt powerful hands pulling him up.

"It's best you come quietly."

Ten minutes later Patterson stood in front of a close-faced Robertson.

"Good to see you again, Mr. Patterson."

"How can I help you?" Patterson replied icily.

"I understand you're returning to Toronto."

"Yes. I have been reassigned."

"Ah yes, the life of a newspaperman. Always a new story to follow."

"Indeed," Patterson answered. "But before I go, you should know about my final dispatch on the strike."

"Go on."

"It's about Alfred Andrews as the principal force behind the strike's defeat."

Robertson's eyebrows rose, then drew together. "Exposure of that nature is inadvisable."

"Why?"

"Andrews will be calling you as a witness in the strike trials."

"Why?"

"I am not at liberty to say. However, I advise you to not make him an enemy."

"I'll take my chances."

"Why don't you write about me instead?"

"Simple. As a public figure your actions will come to light, but Andrews and the Citizens' have been operating in the dark with no accountability."

After several moments of awkward silence, Patterson broke. "Why have you brought me here?"

"Yes. *Why are* you here?" intoned Robertson. "As you have subsequently come to understand, the offer of the Strike Committee contained in the letter which you conveyed to me prior to the leaders' arrests was brought too late. Had it come to my attention earlier, perhaps the more unpleasant consequences of the strike could have been avoided."

"Do you mean State-sponsored violence and terrorism that was responsible for two deaths, dozens of injured men and women, and almost 100 arrests?"

"State-sponsored?"

"RNWMP firing on unarmed citizens, Lewis machine guns mounted on Canadian Army Group vehicles and soldiers with fixed bayonets occupying the city. I was personally involved in a confrontation in Hells' Alley, where armed special police terrorized, attacked and injured innocent men and women. Many were hospitalized."

"Unfortunate consequences, I agree, but Mayor Gray did read the Riot Act and specifically warned women not to be part of Saturday's gathering."

"Perhaps, but shots were fired before he finished reading."

"That's open to interpretation."

Patterson felt his jaw flex angrily. *It is futile to argue with this man.*

"Let us discuss why I wanted to see you."

"Certainly."

"It's about your diary."

"My diary?"

"Yes. It was necessary to confiscate it to ascertain evidence you were conspiring with strike leaders. We have found such evidence."

"I don't believe you! What exactly have you found?"

"Your diary records a meeting with journalist Colonel Graham Davies in which you stated the Strike Committee had a spy in the GNWT office who was providing the Committee with copies of wires forwarded or received about all actions contemplated by the military, their strength and armament."

"So?"

"Failure to share this information with the authorities was a crime. However, there may be a way to avoid criminal proceedings against you."

"A way?"

"It involves the letter from the Strike Committee we discussed prior to the late-night arrests. What do you plan to do with it?"

Patterson had expected Robertson might ask about the letter, and had already made a decision, though it meant giving up an even greater scoop about the strike than the Sokolowski exclusive.

"Nothing. The letter will remain confidential. No one will know of its existence except us."

A look of total surprise came over Robertson's face. "Is the Strike Committee aware of this?"

"No, though I was advised by William Ivens to retain it for my own protection. With so many arrests happening here and my, shall we say, having being acquainted with some of those arrested, it's evidently prudent for me to keep the contents of the letter private unless you plan on arresting me."

Robertson paused for a few moments for effect. Expecting Patterson would thwart his attempt to secure the Strike Committee's unconditional written offer, he had devised a plan. "I can assure you, Mr. Patterson, arresting you for the contents of the diary will not happen as long as the Strike Committee's letter will not be made public."

Patterson smiled. "So if I don't release the letter, there will be no arrest and you will let me report in peace?"

"That is the agreement."

Patterson hesitated. He hated the deal but also did not want to end up in jail, nor stop reporting.

"Do we have an agreement?" pressed Robertson.

"Yes, we do."

"In that case, I will keep your diary."

"And I will keep the letter."

Robertson stood. "Now that we have an understanding, please don't let me keep you any longer. I wouldn't want you to miss your train."

Power corrupts, and absolute power corrupts absolutely, thought Patterson as he left Robertson without a handshake.

An hour later he was on the train, reading a copy of the last issue of the strikers' paper.

On the front page was Dixon's final message to strikers.

```
Get ready for the next fight. Labour must
speak in no uncertain terms at the next
municipal elections. Now is the time to
```

select candidates. Now is the time to begin the campaign. Don't slink to the rear and be slaves. Keep in the forefront of battle. Labour must fight on until she wins the long war for freedom. Never quit. Never say die. Carry on.

The End

Author's Note

*T*he *Reporter and the Winnipeg General Strike* is based on my MA thesis, "The Response of the *Toronto Daily Press* to the Winnipeg General Strike," and my non-fiction books *Winnipeg's General Strike: Reports from the Front Lines* and *The Winnipeg General Strike: Ordinary Men and Women Under Extraordinary Circumstances*.

Washington Post publisher Philip Graham described journalism as "the first rough draft of history." *The Reporter and the Winnipeg General Strike* dramatizes this concept through the firsthand accounts of the strike by *Toronto Advocate* reporter William Patterson — a composite of *Toronto Star* journalists William Plewman and Main Johnson — and *Advocate* publisher Joseph Anderson, who portrays *Star* publisher Joseph Atkinson.

History has proven the *Toronto Star*'s strike coverage was the most accurate, balanced and in-depth of any Canadian newspaper.

— Michael Dupuis
Victoria, 2020

Michael Dupuis is a retired Canadian-history teacher, consultant, writer and author. In 2006 he was a consultant to CBC television for *Bloody Saturday*, in 2011 to CBC television for *Titanic: The Canadian Story* and in 2011 to Danny Schur's documentary *Mike's Bloody Saturday*. In 2012 he contributed to Paul Heyer's *TITANIC Century: Media, Myth and the Making of a Cultural Icon*. In 2014 Michael published *Winnipeg's General Strike: Reports from the Front Lines*, in 2017 *Bearing Witness: Journalists, Record Keepers and the 1917 Halifax Explosion* and in 2018 *The Winnipeg General Strike: Ordinary Men and Women Under Extraordinary Circumstances*. He holds a BA (English) and MA (history) from the University of Ottawa and a BEd from the University of Toronto. An avid pickleball player, Michael resides in Victoria, BC, with his wife Christine and Golden retrievers Piper and Ben. He can be reached at

michaeldupuis@shaw.ca